JULIO ORTIZ

MACHINE

ISBN 978-1-954345-65-2 (paperback)
ISBN 978-1-954345-66-9 (digital)

Rushmore Press LLC
1 800 460 9188
www.rushmorepress.com

Printed in the United States of America

CHAPTER 1

There was a time in the early 2000s when the amount of lawlessness was seen in excess around the world. More particularly near the United States and Mexican border, a lot of crime and violence had stemmed up resorting to firing shed amongst several organizations, all of which are battling out wars over turf and a few hungry souls looking to make a name for themselves. They were people fighting over territory and routes to see who can control the drug trade into the United States looking to line their pockets with American dollars. To add to the situation, poverty in the region was soaring and it seemed as if the best employment or the best way to create an income would be by illegal means. There were also a lot of people willing to do so much for so little. To someone looking in from the outside, it seemed terrifying and disorienting—self-appointed rule by force, chaotic with no agenda—as if everything was being done with very little order. Maybe order was not on the agenda; maybe the hands of those people needed to be tempted to see who would stay. There would be glory returned to the region. There are too many resources here to not find a way to succeed. Its greatest are the people themselves, but who would stay? Who can walk without falling when one is added more and more weight—the pressure, tension, failing economy, scrupulous politicians, and law enforcement? The pressure adds to your legs—tension, the uncertainty of an end to the tunnel, and the doubt in the back of your mind that you may not be strong enough to overcome the situation. Sure, stumbling is allowed. You pick yourself up and continue with the same weight you held before you stumbled, but now your knees have scars and people can look and see you've fallen before. The key is not to think about them and continue walking, and yes, there might be more weight added to your cargo, but if you hang in there long enough, it does get better. Your legs become stronger; your endurance steadier. That temptation sometimes creates fear and you will see that fear is a motivator of several things. It can hold you back from discovering your true potential. A possibility of failure and pain can hold someone back, but it's how you react to it and cope afterward that makes you, especially if you can live with your decision of "almost" made it. That's great. Fear can also be the biggest motivator to amass your strengths and overcome your fears. Some of us think that the pain of living the rest of our lives wondering what could have been far outweighs the pain of being hurt for a moment. We can eventually accept a loss, but the curiosity of never knowing or if only we had done this or that hurts. How do people decide to look the other way or to the unethical? If a bullet could save lives, would it? If people were arrows and shot through a bow, you would know there is a long process in the manufacturing of an arrow. Situations have been just right. Think of launching arrows—some will miss their mark and stray off course. As the archer, you have been trained and steadied, yet the arrow veers from direction and finds its own; some break and split once hitting the bottom, the ground. Every one of those broken arrows had an opportunity for the person to find the target; no one knows why or how it veers off. A sudden gust of wind? Debris on the bow? Or simply the rotation of the Earth? It just happens. The evidence remains. The grains of the wood in the arrow prove to be heavier to one side; it was unbalanced and tumbled to one side, which is why it steers off course to its inevitable end. Some people are too angry; some can never let off any steam. Is there a lesson in the life of that arrow? That balance is key in reaching our own makes— to want things but not too much and not too little. It was evident in the arrow as it is in people. Nothing goes unpunished; nothing goes unseen. What begins when power and greed take a seam and get further mated becomes a myth that no one could have seen coming. Technology has started to govern our interests, mindsets, and lives. It wouldn't be too long before somebody would take that governing image and give it an entity, but it wasn't true. There was no link. Yet, the more people questioned about an entity to have the ability to merge or see technology, the more people began to believe it. They wanted to believe it; they feared the current regimen, wanting to believe there could be a regulator to their regulators—a group or someone who was honest, righteous, and sinecure. No one and no group fit the description, but people started becoming stronger in themselves all over the world—this is that group. These are some of their actions, rises, and falls; there is no membership card and you may have been enrolled your whole life. The trick is who knows that they are and who doesn't.

CHAPTER 2

A series of deaths along the Rio Grande encourages several ranchers to take up arms for protection, which they are entitled to. However, escalating tensions always seem to make matters worse. Drug trafficking, organized crimes, and people smuggling were on the rise within their homestead. People were getting shot and residents would find ways to fight back. The body count kept rising on both sides. Some of the people risking it all were not involved in an organized crime, but they were being hunted south of the border as well. The cartels were using force to persuade anyone and everyone to use their services with their protection at their price. People from near and far seeking a better life had an option to stay and fight or leave and risk it all marching through the valleys of hate. It was a situation no human being should have to put up with. While the Mexican authorities were making no progress, the United States decided to be proactive, granting new funds available to aid Law Enforcement agencies to put more pressure on the war on drugs and defend its border stateside.

Within the ranks of the FBI, there was a young eager agent who had proven to be a good scholar and was looking to make a name for himself as an investigator. Enter Leonardo Cortez—Leo for short. He was in his mid to late 20s, a healthy guy, somewhat of a natural dresser, not too flashy, simple, and occasionally worked out. Ever since leaving the army, his goal had been to become a better agent, doing a lot of grunt work and playing roles on a team that were nothing major. However, he did a very well job at it, memorizing everyone's duties and tasks. He had applied for the role of a lead investigator a few times but had always been rejected. He kind of didn't even really want his job right now, but he went on an interview and they thought he would be a good fit, so he was accepted. His parents were Mexican-Americans. He grew up in Houston, Texas during the late 90s. Attitude and intimidation were everywhere; the worse was when it led to violence. To Leo, sometimes, there was a thin line of judgment when choosing to stick with family or following his friends. As a young kid, he saw the cocaine epidemic firsthand. There used to be a crack house across the street from where his parents lived in the early 90s. Mostly every day, he would meet less fortunate than him who was always willing to do what it takes to get one more score—one more fix. When you notice everyone looking down without being in an exhausted state, you have a sense of morality being lost. Judgment was upheld by only a few elders who still live there, but even them, sometimes, would rather go back inside their house saying, "all is lost." The atmosphere of defeat, empty pride, or macho attitude often would lead decent people into theft or unethical ventures. In his neighborhood, letdown and disappointment were common. It seems like every year, the stakes just kept getting higher. People had a hard time being consistently productive in society. Scores and shams to make money just kept getting bigger and bigger. Too often, they were taken by force. It was not uncommon for new people to move in to be promptly greeted by having a break or vandalized into complying with the current establishment. Small-time gangs wanted to be able to operate and not worry about a good neighbor calling the police. Leo later noticed a pattern that over time, the new neighbors stopped calling the police, realizing that theft and loss were a norm. Then, the gang could operate as usual. One time, Leo even spotted the newly moved-in neighbor helping himself to a bicycle from a convenience store a few blocks down. It had changed them, and three months were all it took. Broad daylight was not safe.

The house that several people went to for drugs in the area was run by an older gangster David "Smoky" DeVries who had a long list of felonies. To him, a decent job was not even a thing. It was impossible.

Besides, he knew so many people that used drugs. He just figured he would convert his grand mom's home where he was court-ordered to live in into a place where people could go and buy them. With his proximity to downtown, Smoky generated a lot of traffic, but he set some rules himself and upheld them at gunpoint—no using on his property and no deals after 9 p.m.—period. So, obviously, every day between 8–9 p.m., he had a line of people waiting to go inside his house. Most of them were lower-income people; some were on their way to party at the bars downtown. Sometimes, nicely dressed people would visit him, and you could hear an argument that Smoky's delivery boy had screwed him. People were always looking for more, even the twelve-year-old delivery boys Smoky had. They would take a little bit off the top attempting to collect enough to the point where they could sell it themselves and make some money. The area would from time to time lose quite a few 6th graders. Smoky was not a guy to play with; no one would give him up. The police all knew but decided to take down people below him and occasionally pursue some above him. How they got that information was beyond anyone. Maybe Smoky was smarter than everyone ever thought. It was bad for the neighborhood and it wasn't long until other people wanted that crack house out of business. The economy was good in the streets amidst guns flying off the shelves just like bullets in the streets. Smoky increased his operations just in case he would have to soon relocate. What came next was a lot of gunfire. Smoky stole from other drug dealers at gunpoint to acquire more product and more money. He also upgraded chemists who were in charge of diluting products with chemicals that reduced the drug in quality but provided more volume. The well-being of the user was not exactly Smoky's priority since he was looking for an exit. Smoky would leave but not before hurting the entire community. A small victory having reclaimed that house made the people think they had won, but what came next was a group of people bidding to take Smoky's place by force. A lot of young people were fans of Smoky and dissected his daily routines to attempt to copy them for themselves one day. Some established partnerships; others just grouped to form gangs. Profits were what everyone wanted. The question was how much of a pie can you live with? Eventually, everyone wanted a larger amount. The risks kept getting bigger and bigger until the neighborhood was restless and hot once again. Some people were quoted as saying, "Hey, remember the good old days when Smoky was here?" Now, Smoky ended up in Portland Oregon. He bought himself a small two-bedroom house in a distant suburb town and an older Cadillac Eldorado. He needed to travel quite a while and hope no one ever came looking for him. He stayed very far away from that life. Smoky became a self-taught barber and got a job at a local barbershop. He had walked away with a little over two million dollars, which is not bad for a street dealer. He kept to himself and very rarely kept company or a conversation for that matter. He blended into his new outdoor life and got used to wearing flannel shirts. After six months, Smoky had really developed his talent for grooming men. Sometimes, he wondered if he ever went to prison if he could get paid for cutting guys' hair in there. He will always be a character. Now, something else Smoky would wonder about was how he could just walk away from all that power. Sure, it was only in a few square blocks of one of the biggest cities in the US, but he knew everyone—who he could trust and who he couldn't. He knew who he could slap around and not. There were some older guys that he felt would put a knife in his back if they ever got the chance. He would smile saying, "Now, you'll never get a chance," but then he would picture them in his mind playing a role like the one he used to have, and he would be bitter for a while. He missed that life, but above everything, Smoky missed all the money he used to make. He made calculations all the time and figured he was losing money. It really wasn't true but he was searching for a reason to go back. Every little negative headline that says related to Houston he thought to himself, "I could've prevented that." All it took was a call with his Grandma who said, "Things have gotten worse," and that was it, he kept a person in charge of his home, said he didn't know when he would be back, and drove off to Texas. He moved back and made some fake bank accounts in other states on his way there making deposits. When he arrived, he was greeted by the police. A detective had him pulled over, then he came out of an unmarked car to ask Smoky some basic questions, "Is this your hand? Who is running this part of town? Where were you?" Smoky had no answers, so he just replied, "I'm here to take control of the city." But the control had been lost, people had died, and his product had lost its attractiveness. Then, there were young guns who had lost older brothers at the hands of Smoky.

Before Leo was fifteen, he had seen three people murdered on his street. One day after gunshots, two men ran through his backyard when the police came by and asked if anyone had seen anything. Leo was willing to cooperate but his dad pulled him away and told him, "You didn't see anything." At the time, Leo felt like a coward; he just didn't feel right; he didn't know why his dad made him say that he didn't know anything. Not that his dad was protecting anyone, but he didn't want to stand out. Leo's grandfather was a Mexican immigrant from just on the other side, Tamaulipas. His grandfather never attended school; he had been working since he was five-years-old, and moving to another country brought along a lot more work. His whole life, he was a laborer. He was retired but since he never had anything worth hanging onto in Mexico, he never went back. Leo's father, Silvestre, was born in an old part of Laredo. They eventually ventured into Houston and decided to make it a home. Although Silvestre learned English and grew up amongst Americans, he never felt like he could truly compete for the education or the jobs that were available out there. He felt like his life was destined to be a secondhand citizen, never doing too much or too little—just enough. Silvestre had a family. He was just a hard worker, the type of guy that puts his head down, does his work, and goes home. In his time, he had been a part of a local Mexican gang. In the early 80s, the hardest thing he did as a youth was trying to convince guys leaving the liquor store to buy them six-packs of beer. There were a lot of confrontations and brawls where maybe someone would end up with a black eye. Maybe if they really didn't like someone, they would put a knife in the tire of their car. Wow. Silvestre was from here. The little house across the street was all he's ever known. He's seen the emergence of the current reality; he knows what is happening now. It's sad he knew the streets were a hard place to learn to become a man. He had lost some friends along the way. Are these acceptable casualties? Does everyone create their own destiny? Silvestre had some pivoting moments himself as he got older. Some guys were boasting of being able to make a lot of money quickly but in the end, there was something he wanted more than money—someone. What kept him from falling that path was Leonardo's mother who made him decide to turn a new leaf and be a good person. He gave it all up, straight-arrow—everyone he knew that could somehow influence him into a life of crime. Unfortunately, he became very well at blocking out the rest of the world. He rarely took part in any activities, distancing himself from the community and even his family. He stopped thinking he could make a difference, but just accepted things as they were—accepted that go-nowhere job, accepted his income, accepted this old house his father had helped him buy and that was in constant need of repair, accepted the crime all around him, and accepted the thought of his kids being raised by the same hand that was slapping everyone else outside. There was nothing he could do. In his mind, this was God's will and he accepted it, but not for his son. Leo was angry. There was too much violence and negativity everywhere—it was brainwashing everyone at school and what had become everyone talked about. Somehow, even the details of the worst crimes that happened just a few hours ago were already being gossiped on school grounds. The gossip involved a group of guys who were waiting for their cousin to be released from jail to take the house that Smoky had come back to work out in. A classmate of his was involved who then was also related to the guy recently released—a guy known as Kilo. The night before, they were involved in killing Smoky and ordering the grandmother to sell them the house as the ultimate sign of taking Smoky's power. It was heart-wrenching news, but in that high school, a lot of kids took it as a way of life. Leo didn't feel it was acceptable. Is this the way it was always going to be? Give in? Go with the flow? Did all the kids feel like him? Anyone at all?

CHAPTER 3

Every mind has a breaking point. When Leo was about seventeen, he had made friends with some guys that were not of the best company. A guy named Alberto Ramon was his childhood friend. They would breed dogs and sell the puppies around town, so people would call him BertDog. He didn't mind occasionally going into the crack house. Leo and Bert wanted to be their own man. Leo had a sense to defy his father and get to know life firsthand, and it wasn't hard to find. It didn't take long before Leo was making more new friends and having fun up to a daily basis. He had ventured into the house across the street, the one that used to belong to Smoky and his grandmother. It became his hangout. They had video games, underage drinking, cocaine, marijuana, women, and although everyone was using drugs, all anyone could talk about were the amounts of money they were making, like they were a class of millionaires drinking daiquiris on the lake. It was the place to be. They talked about other houses all over Houston, about the money that they were making, who works for who, and how they were all connected. They even discussed about the up and comers, who might take a shot at them. How did they know? I guess pillow talk goes a long way. It was always very difficult to get anything by the older crew. They knew everything and apparently were all well connected. Some of them showed to have tight bonds with people they never gave up. You would always hear "I got a guy,"

"My guy heard," or "My guy can do it," then amongst themselves, they had a give and take attitude, like a business "I do *this* but only for *this* in return." Most of them were related but there was always a faint glare when they would say goodbye and walk away with a don't-trust-anyone attitude. They all had private stashes—an angle they could be working on for years. Something Leo did learn in his time hanging out at that house was about who he owed his loyalties to—only himself. People flipped to try to save their own skin all the time. Words meant very little to these guys. What it seems to come down to is what you do and how you do it. Even amongst family, never sell yourself out or compromise your will for anyone. It means not to take a hit or less pay for more work and demand what is right, not a cent more not a penny less. Then, if you know your right, defend it until proven wrong and if you don't feel like they're taking care of you, walk away. You start taking stuff and accepting less like if you're on probation working long hours. Years go by and before you know it, you'll be too afraid to go ask your boss at the local grocery store for a 50 cent raise. You'd rather quit, go somewhere else, and start all over again. You talked yourself out of it and that is where you defeat yourself—by not thinking you deserve it. Truth is you do. Work needs compensation and risk needs compensation too, but the easiest thing to do would be to feel uncomfortable about your deal, botch the operation, and end up at that table wearing a wire all because you didn't have the grapefruits to ask or stick up for yourself to make a deal for correct compensation.

Sad truth that most of the boys in the neighborhood just grew older but never became men—easier said than done. Leo would hear stories about other drug dealers' rise and fall throughout the city. It seemed that their common mistake was not believing in themselves, giving up too soon, or putting someone else before themselves. Greed, hot headedness, and sheer psychotic behavior would get them, too. None of these guys grew up perfect but accepting situations and making something were what the older ones knew how to do. Lack of discipline always got guys and women in trouble too. Most of the times, discipline was handled privately but some people are hard to control; things would get out of hand. He heard stories of brothers turning against brothers over money; wives ashamed to visit their husbands in prison because they were not strong enough to resist temptation; guys who were regular Don Juan's with the ladies going to prison then becoming gay. It's okay if they did. There weren't too many people going to visit them to verify and any girl that would have probably didn't. Maybe it's just lies to stay away from them. It's always hard to believe the drastic changes. People do hard things in desperation but those would be the lucky ones. Other guys would commit suicide for a girl that just wasn't into them, because they lost some money, or looking at a long sentence tough to be able to conquer and accomplish so much but they feel empty and can't have what money cannot buy.

For BertDog and Leo, life was good times smoking weed and talking to girls. BertDog was into making money. Leo had a girl that he liked; she was cute, easy on the eyes. They lived nearby. Leo had always teased her as she used to wear glasses when she was younger. They seemed to have put that behind and got along except Leo never really saw himself having a relationship with her, although they were inseparable. Sometimes, it almost seemed like he was being set up to see her. There were occasions he was invited to places and she would be there. He liked her, but he had aspirations. There were more things that he wanted from this life. He had no clue what, but he genuinely felt like he had to figure it out on his own. Maybe everyone has that desire, and for Leo, he was convinced he would act on it. One day, a friend of his caught him off guard and asked him, "Hey, so are you going to hook up with her?" Leo looked shocked by the question. "No," he replied. Then the guy asked, "Don't you wish that girl would move away? Or go to jail or something?" Leo said, "Naw man, jail is too harsh. If she moves away, that would be fine. It will give me a chance to meet someone else. It seems like everywhere I go, there she is." The guy looked at him and chuckled. In the upcoming weeks, quite a few guys that were regulars started getting arrested. The police stopped asking Leo and his family for any help probably because they already knew the answer.

One day at school, a guy Leo knew asked him to do a favor that could get him in trouble. Leo said, "Sure." The guy handed him a snub nose 38 revolver wrapped in a handkerchief, told him to hold it for him for a few days, to act like nothing was wrong, not touch it, and that soon, he would ask for it back. Leo agreed. It was the longest day of his school life. Things got even worse because students started talking about another student who had taken a gun to school and was planning on using it. The guy who they were talking about eventually broke under pressure and gave himself up or stood out too much after everyone was talking about it. There was a search for the weapon but amongst so many students, it was going to take too long. The police were everywhere. His bookbag was found but there was no gun. Leo was pale white as he exited the building all the time being watched by the guys who handed it to him. They were suspects but denied everything, even taking the bookbag in the first place. Leo walked home as he always did. He felt like a drug mule but blocked everything out and kept on going. *What if he's stopped and they find the gun in his possession? What if the other kid claims Leo as the true attempted shooter at school that day?* Leo regrouped, regained his composure, and kept pace, ice in his veins. Patrol cars would pace right behind him as he walked. Other patrol cars would turn onto the street he was walking on and flare the siren quick. Maybe if Leo ran, he was done. Leo kept his cool and pace. His palms were sweaty. He finally made it home, pulled out the wrapped gun, and placed it in between his mattress where he believed it to be safe. The following days, no one mentioned anything about any gun or shooting attempt. Just a weird lonely guy who must have been having a bad day on meds or whatever he was taking flipped out and was taken to wellness hospital. Leo thought himself a hero but couldn't say anything. The emotions in him were through the roof, and nobody knew what almost happened. Well, except for the guys that stole it and gave it to Leo, but how did they know? Leo looked for them, but they refused to direct their gaze at him or acknowledge he was there. Leo didn't know what to do, and in the days that followed, he looked for ways of detecting a gun on an assailant using electrical equipment. The whole notion fascinated him. This was spy tech, but the guys who handed the gun to him aren't this sophisticated. How did they know? Leo was unaware of this that day, but that episode in his life sparked a quality in him that would lead him to his destiny, and it all started with his curiosity. The down side is that several days went by and Leo still possessed the gun. It would call to him and tempt him to hold, touch, and disassemble it. It got the better of him, so he did. Finally, he went outside with the gun tucked in the back of his jeans. He threw out his chest and walked with a strut as if his shoulder were too heavy for his body and he had to swing them from side to side to maintain balance. He felt invincible, even gave off a partial one-sided grin like no one could mess with him. What he failed to notice was everyone turning and looking at him shaking their heads, saying, "What's wrong with this boy?" Then Leo's friends stopped talking to him except BertDog. He went by late one night and before he left, he said, "No clowning with that piece, okay! Or it's your ass." Weird because Leo didn't mention he had it nor what he had been doing with it. The whole situation was weird and out of place. It just kept getting weirder when his dad was sent home from work and came home in a very grumpy mood that never happened then. His father lectured him that day. He told him, "Leo, my son, there's nothing stronger than family. Friends come and go. You always have to look out for yourself. Understand that when it's all said and done, all your actions will only belong to you." Leo never asked questions but maybe he should. Why was there a gun in his house? What had he to do with any of it? What Leo failed to see was right in front of his eyes. The streets were hot. He was supposed to be on his best behavior but was failing. It was getting dark. He knew where the guy who handed him the gun lived. He knocked on the door for about five minutes before his sister came and told him, "He's not here, he's at the arcade inside the convenience store four blocks away." "Thank you," he said as he threw his hoodie over his head and started walking to the store. It was a cool night, low temperature. As he was walking over there, a lot of people came out from their house just to witness him walking by. Leo did not have the gun on him, but he did notice the people and thought "very strange." Leo arrived and went inside the convenience store. There were two police officers paying for their soft drinks and soon walked out. Leo walked all around that store, but the guy was nowhere to be found. No one was at the video games. The store also had gas pumps. As Leo left, he recognized a few of them pumping gas from the crack house—four older guys that had recently been released from jail. For some reason, Leo waved at them. As he went by, they had a blank look on their face. They just kept staring back at him so intensely it intimidated Leo from asking for the whereabouts of his friend, so he kept on walking home. As soon as he left, gunshots went off. Those same guys had gone inside the convenience store and robbed the place. Now, Leo panicked. He had practically started running away, why? He was not guilty. He did not even think of how it looked. He was afraid. The only thing rushing through his head was what his dad had told him earlier—to just look out for himself. When he got home, he felt betrayed by his friend like he had been set up to be inside and arrested along with them. Leo took the gun out from where he had placed it, went to a park, and threw it away in the garbage can. Of course, Leo had been seen and it didn't take long to find out who the gun belonged to—the father of the kid who was recently released from wellness and prescribed medication. Answers were being uncovered. The following day, an investigator came knocking on his front door. He was questioning Leo about the robbing at the convenience store because he was identified on the video footage being there just moments prior and did not purchase anything, and also about a snub-nosed 38 revolver that was found in a garbage can at a nearby park and was recovered that morning. No one verified Leo as being the person leaving it there. He was smart enough to wipe off his fingerprints but the owner's son and him do go to the same school. Decision-making time—what was Leo going to do? Who did he owe loyalty to? The investigator was very firm and showed no sign of compassion. If Leo chose to defend those guys he waved at, he was ready to take Leo downtown and book him for the whole robbery. Multiple people saw him on his way there, and running away. There was a footage of Leo waving at the suspects moments before they stormed in. Who knew such a simple gesture as waving hello to someone could cost you so much? His friend was unseen and unheard of at least by him. Leo started to panic even now. Maybe as in every human being, their own survival shoots to the top of their priorities. He would feel like a coward again for all the right reasons. He said the truth and told the investigator about his friend bringing the gun to him during class hours at school for no reason and threw it into the garbage can. By the time the questions moved to the robbery, Leo was nearly in tears and said, "Yes, I know those guys from the crack house across the street. I had no idea what they were going to do. All I did is wave. I swear I'm not in it. I didn't know. I'm telling you the truth." The detective already had most of the pieces. Those boys were tight with long lists of acquaintances and Leo was not among them. However, he had just thrown his school friends under the bus. I guess it is true. All friendships end in betrayal. The investigator advised Leo's father to "Get Leo out of town" and what the investigator said next rings in his memory even to this day: "Jail is too harsh for him. Maybe just move him away."

Within twenty-four hours, Leo was on his way to live with his aunt Betty in Chicago. Now, although the crime was just as equal in Chicago as it was in Houston, Leo was somewhat starting over so he mostly kept to himself. He felt like he had dodged the bullet. He felt in some way like a guy who knew his way around the streets and how wrong he was. Houston was educating him. He just couldn't see it that there was a purpose. It takes strength to say the truth and to stand up for yourself even if it hurts and then lose the people you care about. Leo would have flourished. He deserved to be in his hometown walking in the light, righteous. Moving away isolated him, gave him a lot of discipline, taught him to find himself, to find strength within, to not need anything but work for what you do want, and to enjoy it once achieved.

He took up boxing and made friends with a guy who was about ten years older than him, Arthur Garcia, a tough guy who had served in the army and was currently in school to become a police officer. Leo's interest slowly grew into the possibility of himself being a police officer like his friend Arthur. Arthur would always say that the hardest part is learning to restrict yourself as discipline he loved to fight. Leo would be greatly influenced by him, pick up his traits, graduate school, and enroll in the military himself finding that he had capabilities he thought not possible. He proved to be a good student even when the time came to get creative or come up with different approaches to old tasks. He excelled as he saw things differently. Leo smiled more and was having a good time. He would also get a chance to make friends throughout the country, learn new lifestyles, travel to remote places in the US, and visit some of those exotic places overseas he had only read about. Every year, he felt stronger. He was being groomed a modern soldier and educated to stand proper off the base and in front of the world as a gentleman. Some people would say he was pretending to be something he was not because he did not come from an entitled family. To Leo, it felt right and good to progress and grow—to win awards based on hard work. The worst part were the letdowns of coming in second. The hardest critic of his shortcomings was always himself. Tough loss—only to him. He returned to Chicago earning a police officer in the same precinct as his friend Arthur. He was doing a very good job, but he wanted more. He applied for the process to become an FBI agent. He was appointed to an FBI branch in Dallas, Texas where he excelled at every task he was assigned to. He became a very good group participant but again, he wanted more when a spot came up in Houston as a lead investigator. He called in as many favors as he could to try and get that job. There were pros and cons to having Leo fill that position—he was still young, but he had proven himself to be capable. Maybe, he would serve as a beacon to illuminate the way for those who were younger than him to strive or for the older ones who thought they had lost their way in life a spark of guidance. Houston was Leo's hometown and his story had been silenced all these years. Some who believed him to be in prison or dead—how would they react? Would they even care? If it encourages just one person to get off their butts and do something positive for themselves, it's a win. Some people believe that there is no hope, that no one makes it out and succeeds. Fate brought Leo back to Houston.

CHAPTER 4

For a few months, nothing was new—usual arrests and lone assailants looking for a way to get by out of every day desperation. People using drugs seemed to get younger and younger as well as the one selling them. People who were genuinely evil didn't last. They were a different type of criminal—reckless and destructive. Their peers usually cast them out and avoid them, so sometimes, you would find them where no one was. Leo was doing well at his new job. He was flourishing. It only took six months for Leo to start seeing patterns and similarities in crimes—where people went to perform them and the odd crimes no one expected were trickier, but Leo managed to unravel them no matter how cleaver the suspect was. These people showed to have a lot of discipline, patience, and book smart character, even knowing the patterns of the county forensic specialist just from reading novels or books, describing their work, and what they look out for. These people showed to be good, honest, and hard-working people, so what would lead them into committing a crime? A weakness? Fall into temptation? Was it overthinking a situation into believing it is their only option? There is always an option. The hardest one is walking away. Praise the people that do even if we never hear about them. Good. Leo proved to be an efficient investigator and even helped around the community. He was not the type of guy to dwell or be ashamed of his humble roots. To him, he owed the city something more than just his civic duty. He found out that shortly after he left the town, the crack house across the street was closed. It was not really a topic of conversation and when he reached out to his parents, they already moved outside of the loop and into the western suburbs, in a nice town called Katy. The crack house was empty for some years in foreclosure and eventually, someone bought that home at a very good price, fixed it up, then sold to a nice young family. The location was prime and the surrounding streets were a lot cleaner than what Leo remembered. The neighborhood looked better—kids would play outside again and now, it even looked prosperous. His friend BertDog had also left the town and was never heard from again. Those guys who handed him the gun at school, neither was held up on that day for that incident, but out of the four, two of them got better and led very productive lives; two of them wasn't very fortunate. Leo could have dug a little deeper and found all their true whereabouts but decided not to. He was in a good place, advancing in his career, and crossing his T's and dotting his I's. He had been tested and had chosen the righteous path—not too concerned about being rich or owning an island, but just living well and helping people out. Sure, he continued to be tempted and all the time even when he was out drinking at the local bar where his friends would pressure him into another one. However, Leo had a good willpower and seemed very optimistic in life. Whatever came next and whatever form it happened, Leo could confront it and was already ready to accept the consequences. As straight a shooter, you would find the Houston Bureau.

One day, Leo was specifically focusing on a case where people had been found assassinated outside Laredo. From the eight bodies, six were Houston natives. All eight had key parts of skin removed on their arms and some of them in the neck area. The way they were found suggested they were dumped at the location and had been decomposing for several days. Leo did not have a hard time finding the identity of these people. On the youngest of all the deceased, Leo identified him from a recent juvenile detention file that had his picture years before, which is perhaps from the first time the deceased was placed into juvenile detention. Leo wanted to make sure before he had to inform a loving family that their son had died, so he worked with sketch artists and the coroner's office to come up with sketch of what the youngest deceased might've looked like. Then, he flipped through pictures of him to inmates and people on the outside who might have known him, trying to inquire on his whereabouts and determine who he was. What was he doing in Laredo? What tattoo or design had been near surgically removed or cut out from his skin? No one helped him. Some of the other bodies had tattoos naming streets in Houston on them but it seemed like removing their skin was removing a crucial identifying mark. Out of ten people that could have given Leo a lead or information, nobody wanted to talk about him. Nobody said anything, not even for a reduction of sentence or for the tease of a get-out-of-jail free card. Leo's patience with these people was worn out, so he resorted to another tactic to find out who Sam was and who he hung around with, which left Leo tracing back Sam's steps and looking for cameras where Sam may have been presented a daunting task. Sam had been released from Juvenile Detention five months ago but once he exited the building, the street camera feed from the day Sam was released was inaccessible. However, Leo found a payment on his mother's debit card from that day just two hours later. His mother had stopped at a small restaurant and paid using her debit card but there was no online camera feed for that inside the small diner. All Leo needed to do was visit the restaurant, see if they had cameras, and review the footage. It was a long shot to capture anything useful and maybe even nothing would come up but it's his job to investigate it, so he made the two-hour drive. Luckily, they did record the camera feed onto VHS, deleted, and taped over the film every six months. It was a small taco diner and luckily, one camera showed Sam, his mother, and a teenage girl having lunch that day. He bought the film and completed sketches of the girl that was with them. Sam had no sisters and at seventeen years of age, Leo was betting that the girl and the deceased had a personal relationship. Leo went through the pictures of high school students at the high school Sam was supposed to go to and concluded that the girl in the video was Angela Watson. Leo decided whether or not to question her if she knew Mr. Sam Luna starting with the basics then with the complicated questions to see if she could possibly shed some light. He went through the legal process necessary to bring her in for questioning. She blew them off and didn't show. He could have her arrested or go through the legal system on a much harder route that may have ramifications since he really didn't know what the deceased was doing. Maybe she blew him off because she was involved and he just didn't know. Angela was a seventeen-year-old young woman who worked part-time at a strip mall retail store. Leo decided to go buy something and maybe ask her a question or two just to test the waters and see what happens. Leo went inside and did not initially see her. He asked the manager and said she took a small break and will be back shortly. Leo walked about two stores over into a coffeehouse and caught a glimpse of a girl resembling Angela doing her homework with her head buried into her study material. He approached the area where she was sitting and caught a glimpse of her bookbag with multiple pictures of her and Sam on it. One of them had a picture of Sam wearing a sleeveless shirt hugging her and he could see the tattoo that was removed. It resembled something that looked like a machine's electric circuit schematic. "Hi, how are you?" She did not even bother looking up—probably didn't think anyone would approach her or talk to her after a pause. She must've noticed because she said, "Hey," then followed it up with, "You know, whatever you're selling, I really don't want any." Leo smirked, "Miss Angela Watson, I'd like to ask you a few questions about a guy named Sam Luna. Do you know him?" She looked up, seemed a little bit nervous, grabbed her stuff, and began to get up from the table. "I was just enjoying some coffee, looked up, and happened to see you. My name is Leo Cortez, FBI. I'm working on a case I believe you might know something about that could help us bring peace to Sam and his loved ones. Anything will be helpful." She refused to give Leo any of her time and started packing up angrily. "I have to go. You don't look like an FBI. Where's your badge?" He reached into his back pocket and showed her. She saw it then turned the other way as if she had just been disappointed. "Well, maybe you are an FBI but I have anything to tell you. You'll never arrest him." He very arrogantly said, "He's dead." She turned to face him as if she could decipher his facial expression into knowing the truth, then her look was overcome with sadness. Leo replied, "I'm sorry, I believe it to be him. When was the last time you saw him? What was he doing? What was he into?" She had tears running down her face. "Tuesday . . . no, no, you're lying. This is a cop's game. He's not dead. He's too strong and too smart. Please stay away from me." She hurried out of the coffee house. Leo felt terrible, but he felt like he could shed light on the who-thing by looking into Sam Luna. It is sensitive because he was young but some of the older guys may not report to any of their family, possibly not in years. Leo decided to create or pursue other leads. He needed to release Sam to the family, then the mother verified the body to be her son. Angela would have to step forward with any information on her own but there was no way Leo would hold his breath until she stepped forward. It was also possible she didn't know anything, so Leo moved on with the investigation. He started identifying and following the leads on the rest of the dead bodies. Leo began to suspect that the tattoos had something to do with the murders although it was a common thing for people to have tattoos especially in his line of work where tattoos were often affiliated to a gang or belonging to certain groups of belief. However, tattoos are also mostly for self-expression and individualism, so Leo visited a few tattoo parlors, talked with artists, and see if he could get any information to a person, a place, or a group that may abide to similar-looking tattoos, looked at websites of tattoo designs and photo, and inquired on a few similar to the one he saw on Angela's notebook, but nobody gave him anything solid. It all said it was just a personal preference. Leo went to the local HPD Gang Investigations Unit and specifically requested files but they seemed to be from all types of people—completely random with no pattern or proximity to any location. Did a new church form underground that everyone was aware of but anyone in the law enforcement? When Leo asked the detectives on the Gang Unit about what they thought of the circuit imagery tattoos, they replied, "Yes we've seen them. Doesn't mean anything like having a heart, sports logo, or a care bear drawn on you."

Leo was not convinced. He found files at the local Wellness Hospital containing pictures of circuit tattoos. His name is Jose Cruz, a once prominent college football star who became a used car salesman, married four times, and admitted into the Mental Hospital three times. Leo was denied a visit with the patient for his questions may startle him, so Leo requested a copy of all the files and images they had with Mr. Cruz. Apparently, Mr. Cruz believed his phone was talking to him and caught him cheating every time he did something bad. It would also reward him, or so he claimed, every time he did something good for someone. The bad seemed to win more often than the good. It was weakening Mr. Cruz but it was diagnosed on every occasion to be just in his mind—his phone does not control his life. Mr. Cruz also made an allegation of an army being built, that he had to prove himself worthy of being accepted by the way he acted, not by anything he said. His words didn't mean anything; it was determined by what he did if he would be worthy entering the kingdom of the machines, through circuits. When asked for proof of this alleged army, Mr. Cruz could not provide any. Again, the diagnosis was that he was being overworked and needed to slow down, go on a vacation, take three weeks off, and rebuild. Mr. Cruz on his last visit claimed the army was real and a leader would be chosen by the internet to be in its physical form amongst us, an entity he referred to as the Toolmaker, also claiming, "It could be anybody." Just remembering or being in the real world with any form of these illusions would cause Mr. Cruz to go into a crazed panic. He genuinely believed it. Relief and immunity of those thoughts came from quiet time at the Wellness Hospital. Could these men found near Laredo be members of such an army? Be the leader? But executed? An opposing faction? Mr. Cruz may have had years of weasel behavior that could cause a man to lose himself very easily. A sleazy person becomes weak mentally without wanting to. Everyone knows they want to be good and survive, but doing bad on purpose has an element. It's only a matter of time until you give up or get caught; they'd be afraid the party won't last forever. It's always fear of having their con brought to the light or another smarter to pull a con on their con. Then, there's the approach of the mob. Once they discover your con, no, don't stop, keep going, but now there's something on you—blackmail.

On the surface, Jose Cruz lived beyond his earnings. Major dept, he would have spurts and moments of great wealth, or he could have multiple salesman of the month awards, but the evidence proved he had not had one in over a year. He was popular. Several people knew who he was, but Leo wanted to concentrate on a few friends who might really know him. His research paid off. The people Leo questioned were truly saddened to see him deteriorate as they claimed, "It seems like when he's dating a woman, he's winning. He can't lose. Everything's going for himself, then he marries her, and the problems start. Before you know it, he has a mistress. Then, he starts losing money. Jez, he's a handsome guy, great family. You'd think that after four tries, he'd see his mistakes. Hope he gets better." Then, Leo asked some of his former wives about Mr. Cruz. The last ex-wife, the one who was with him when he first went into the hospital, sums it up very well. She said, "He's like the Michael Jordan that never made it. Oh, very competitive. A true go-getter but always looking for the next one and the next one—a little bit bigger, a little bit shinier. And sometimes, he realizes he's not Michael Jordan. What he has means nothing. He'll throw it all away and move on to find a new conquest, a new chase. Everything's never enough." Leo wanted to know of his morals or personality so he asked, "Is Jose one to bend the rules to get what he wants?" She replied, "Oh no, maybe he changed. He works hard but to him, working twice as hard will get him there in half the time. I don't know if he can be happy. He'd have to become Donald Trump, but even then, Jose would probably want more." Leo recorded every word she was saying. Then, he asked, "When he was admitted the first time, he had tattoos but no robot circuit tattoos, then the second and third time and he seemed to have gotten more and more, can you tell me anything about them?" She was an honest woman saying, "Mr. Cortez, I wouldn't know about the second or third but when he was released after the first time, he would stray from his meds, feel good about himself, and forget the hospital thing ever happened then start up all over again. It's who he was—competitive—erase your loses and move on, get done, get rich, or die trying. He claimed somehow to have met a group of people that could help him get rich, but he needed to give up working at the dealer. He did, but he did not get rich. It was a huge let down. He went back to the dealer, then started getting money from the group that hired him to do home refinance referrals to his friends and people he knew, so he gives up the dealer again, then again nothing happened. Of course, he would lose his mind with all of this back and forth. But with all this extra time, he was more at the gym and when I suspected he was seeing someone, he denied it, and the worst thing I ever did was stay with him for another six months when we were going broke. Suffocated. One day, being fed up, I confronted him again and he had built up enough courage to tell me the truth—he had a girlfriend. I took my daughter and left that house. I finally left him and the next day, I got a promotion with a bonus at work. The robots, he would call me every day at ten thirty at night talking about someone telling him to call me. It's not true, then he started saying that he could lead some robot army if he acted right, like a gentleman. That's when I changed my number and everyone's who he might've called. The divorce soon after finalized. He's a good man. In college, he witnessed a car accident and got burned while retrieving someone who was left inside the car. He was the star tight end and missed the big playoff game because he wouldn't get released from the hospital until 6 p.m. The game finished at 7 p.m. The team lost the game. He believes in himself that he is that good and that kind of guy. Maybe he knows it and feels sorry for himself for the missed opportunities, making up for it by completing some big score that may or not ever come. This robot leader stuff sounded crazy. It would not surprise me if his desperation has caused him to raise the stakes. I knew it sounded illegal." She thought Leo had arrested him, so he told her of the case he's investigating. "Did you ever meet anyone he hangs out with that may have these robot tattoos?" She smiled. "He's popular, knows people all over the country, he's an easy talker even though most of what he says is bullshit. I can't recall, sorry."

Mr. Cruz did very little to help with Leo's case but nonetheless, he noted Mr. Cruz's statements on the board. Leo needed more resources, so he requested information from his colleagues in Austin and Dallas and decided to pick their mind to see if they knew anything of these robot tattoos or circuit board designs. The only thing they said was they would call him if they got anything. Leo had been bitten by the curiosity bug. He put his own artistic talents to use and was able to simulate Sam Luna's design and staple it to the wall in his office. Some time went by and day by day, he would receive more and more files and reports associated with robot circuit tattoos. Leo stopped for a while, appeared at court, and testified on behalf of the state of Texas one day and while he was helping with the corrections officer with the receiving of an inmate from the County, he noticed a second inmate who had a similar circuit board tattoo. The inmate he was receiving claimed to have no knowledge of who that second inmate was and he had no incentive to cooperate with the arresting FBI agent who was moments away from testifying against him. Afterward, Leo was able to make a few phone calls and find out the name of that second inmate, even earning a chance to ask him a few questions. His name was Lester Myrtle. It was his second time going to jail for domestic battery, a twenty-two-years-old local kid. Once Leo got a chance to ask him what the meaning of the tattoos is, he said, "We all need help. We all want to become better." Leo creeped in and said, "What do you mean?" Then Lester said, "Look, man, I used to pray to God but the only thing that ever got me was a longer detention. It doesn't work. I'm an ugly guy. I found my wife online, technology came through. That's more than God ever did for me. I guess the hard part now is trying to keep her." Leo looked shocked with a bit of anger toward him, "So, you hit her?" Lester was also startled, "I'm not a machine. I'm a human being. Sometimes I overreact, overthink, and sometimes, I don't even trust myself. You know this is going to sound silly but sometimes, I ask for things and they happened. I find advice and guidance online. I learned to cope and deal with issues online. I know I'm not perfect, but technology does help." Leo could not believe what he was hearing—cult fanatics or perhaps just weak people looking for guidance—so he pressed on, "Your phone tells you to hit her your wife?" "*No.*" "Did your phone ever ask you to participate in a crime or commit one?" "*No.*" "So, you hit her on your own will?" There was a lot of tension amongst both men. "Look, man, I got court in a couple of days. I can't tell you why or how, but I guess it happened." Leo attempted to regroup himself, "Do you know anyone else with robot circuit tattoos?" Lester agreed, "I had a friend who wasn't as lucky as me. He thought technology was evil, that it was making him do bad stuff. He ran a red light one day and slammed into a semi. They later found he was tripping really bad. Probably would have died." Lester did not look affected by what he had just said, so Leo asked, "So you're saying his phone pushed him into committing suicide?" shaking his head. "I don't know, man. He went to a very dark place too fast. He started quoting Hitler and made a lot of friends who were also going down that road. Some of them cleaned up, some didn't. To me, it was good, like an awakening I wanted, an awakening I had asked for. About a month after my friend Tommy passed, I proposed to Cindy and it really made me think about the greater picture, you know, life is too short. I still miss him." Leo was a bit moved, then asked, "What is the full name of your friend that died?" Then Lester completed, "Thomas McCrea." "How long ago was this?" "He passed two years ago." Leo wrapped up his files and the recording device. "Thank you, Lester." Leo was impressed having a firsthand account of someone with a robot circuit tattoo. Although he hated Lester's decision making, he acknowledged it was helping the guy. There are always decisions that one must make for the future's sake. People do feel careless until they notice that things are for real. Usually someone gets a speeding ticket, knock up a girlfriend, and worst case, get a DUI. No one wants to see people's lives end; no one wants to see extreme measures taken; we always want to help everyone out. The truth is it's up to everyone to help themselves. Trains are very hard to stop once they get going. Leo said to himself that it is just fate. Tommy's death could in no way be provoked to unite Lester and Cindy. He was over thinking and exhausted, so he tossed the folder underneath the rest of his work and gave up for the day. He was done.

CHAPTER 5

One day, walking by a colleague's desk, Leo noticed an article on his screen talking about a Lester Myrtle who was released from jail due to his girlfriend dropping all charges but not before he received a beating at the hands of two assailants who were not identified in the article at the local Harris County Jail. Leo went back to his office, searched for the file, picked it up, and started reading all over again. The Harris County Jail had since released the two assailants. They claimed to send over their files immediately, but nothing ever arrived. Leo was able to find several files belonging to the deceased Thomas McCrea who was arrested for underage drinking, disorderly conduct, public intoxication, and attempted battery in a shopping mall. But there were also names of people who were with him on these multiple events, so he picked out a few of the names of the people that apparently have gone straight and decided to visit them to see what he could learn of Thomas McCrea in the enigma of the robot tattoos. He decided to focus on two of Thomas' friends, a Janet Cantu and a Mike Sanchez. He decided to visit Janet first as it was a Saturday and he had another appointment afterward in North Houston, so he thought it would take some time out of his workday. However, things didn't quite go according to plan. He knocked on the door and the person that opened was Janet herself but once he identified himself as an FBI agent, she nearly flung the door in his face and asked him to leave, then he said, "I just want to ask you a few questions about Thomas McCrea." She said, "Why would you care now? You're FBI, right? You killed him. It was you. Please don't ever come here again. I'll call the cops. My uncle is HPD. We trust them." Leo took the loss, went back to his car, and decided to take a different approach. Leo made some phone calls and was able to track down who her uncle was—a patrolman by the name of Henry Cantu. That same afternoon, he was able to get a conversation with him. Turns out on one of the arrests of Thomas, he resisted it and was punched in the nose by a man claiming to be an off-duty FBI agent. That info was nowhere in any of the files. Henry himself thought the kids made it up or he fell and bumped his face on the floor looking for a scapegoat, so they blamed the FBI. There was no concrete evidence, but that did not stop them from believing that the FBI had a personal grudge against Thomas McCrea. Henry himself asked Leo to give it some time before he attempted another visitation. Janet and Thomas had been friends since grade school. Mike Sanchez was a full five-years older than most of them. He was a graduate of the Art Institute Houston, making a name for himself as a DJ. Leo was able to obtain his phone number from a DJ listing site, which included Mike's cell number and they arranged a meeting at a coffeehouse. Leo informed him on the first contact that he was an FBI agent and that he wanted information about Thomas McCrea. Mike agreed to cooperate and accepted the invitation. Leo walked into the coffee house not before doing some research on Mike. His parents owned a convenience store and a saloon which they rented out for family parties. Mike excelled as a musician, he looked great, had a good physical condition, and dressed trendy yet had facial hair that did not conform with modern society—perks of belonging in his line of work. Leo took a seat, signaled for the waitress, and Mike began the conversation. "So," he said, "Two years later, someone's finally looking into my friend's murder?" Leo was glad for the conversation. He switched his recording device on and pointed to it as if asking for Mike's permission to record. Mike nodded up and down. Leo said, "Alright, what do you think happened?" Mike replied, "You guys didn't like him, manipulating the lights on that street corner to have him killed." Leo started, "I can assure you that didn't happen." Mike went on and said, "Oh yeah, I was with Tommy earlier that day and he wasn't even that high. He wasn't suicidal, so something happened, someone killed him. I never looked too much into it because I have nowhere to look." Mike was a strong person. It seemed to be a touchy subject but he remained unflinching. Leo said, "I'm sorry, he and a friend of his, named Lester, had these types of tattoos. What can you tell me about them?" showing him a few pictures from a file he brought along with him. "What? The bot circuit tats, they look cool AF that's it." Leo asked, "Do you have any?" Mike replied, "Sure, I do. I got multiple ones like this one at the circuit board in the shape of music notes." Mike pulled up his sleeve to show him. "I mean, yeah, I got it because it looks cool and this is what I love, music. It helps me. It keeps me honest." Leo pointed to a camera as if asking for permission to photograph Mike's arm. He nodded up and down agreeing so Leo took the picture with a digital camera, then asked, "What do you mean?" Mike rolled his sleeve back down then glanced upward as if searching for his response in the sky, then he said, "It's almost like being devoted to one thing and representing it wherever you go, even though yeah, I've noticed when I turn away from music, things turn away from me. These tats on my arms remind me what my goal is, and yeah, I've been tested. I've been offered more money to do something else, but this is it, man. Living the dream." Leo agreed with Mike's statement, then he asked, "Have you ever been offered money in exchange for a crime or a criminal activity?" Mike said, "I'm a DJ. Sometimes, people pay me in cash. I don't ask where it's from. I don't need to know. I don't want to know. Sometimes, I'll do a small favor for them. Sometimes I will, sometimes I won't." Leo tried to push the envelope a little bit further, "Would you be willing to testify against anyone in a court of law regarding these favors? Maybe someone else with these types of tattoos?" He looked startled wondering why Leo even asked that question, then he replied, "Look, man, it's bizarre but the people I meet with these tattoos are good, hard-working, and honest people. It doesn't matter how they got their money. Now, the stories I hear about the FBI—double-dipping, playing both sides, intimidating, and harassing people when they're weak—that is true evil." Mike believed that the people he met were not criminals. The latter not believing in law enforcement could mean his lines were blurred. Does he know who the good guys are? Leo's cup of coffee arrived. He gave the waitress a gesture with his lips silently saying, "Thank you." Then, he focused again on Mike and begun, "You're lost, Mike, if you don't know who the good guys are." Mike was a little heated. "Oh, I know who the good guys are. The ones who are happier." Leo decided not to keep arguing with him as he may need help in connection to other cases that Mike may have access to information for. After a while of non-subject-related talk, Mike and Leo seemed to see eye to eye. Mike opened and said, "You know what, Leo, some gossip came out of Laredo." Leo looked surprised as if this was the first time he had heard of it, "Oh, like what?" Mike leaned toward Leo. "I heard that the FBI would not make an arrest on those eight people because they were the ones that killed them, then they sent a rookie golden boy to clean up the leftovers." Leo didn't know how much Mike knew or if he had been instructed to say this to him. He needed to keep the boat in the water and see where the stream leads, so he went along with it and asked, "Why are you telling me this?" Mike replied, "Your famous people around here know you. Heck, some might even like you. Everyone knows where you grew up. I want to see you do good, but I don't think the tattoos have anything to do with anything. It's art, not a prison number. Tommy's been gone. I've lost other good friends. If they aren't here, only their actions are to blame. It always creates reflection into my own life. Leo, take some advice. Stop digging. You might not be able to pull yourself out of the hole. It changes people and not always for the better." Leo was stubborn. He didn't believe Mike but he admired Mike's words of protection, then said, "I'll keep that in mind." Leo got up and left. As he was driving to the office, everything kept playing over in his mind—the back and forth, the sudden answer then none, and the give and go. He even began to believe he was being manipulated. The worst was the accusation about FBI agents assassinating those eight gang members and dumping them outside of Laredo. The whole thing smelled funny. Who was spreading this? Leo had a feeling that the more he asked, the more it might make him seem guilty. The lines were beginning to look blurry even to him. But then, Leo would snap out of it. It was just in his mind. He knows he's on the side of good, working to protect the people, doing his best to uphold the law. The leads grew cold for a few days—nothing toward this case. It seems he would have to wait.

CHAPTER 6

Leo was doing better. He was eating well, working out, and was even meeting a nice girl who he would go out dancing with on the weekend. He was no longer doing too much nor thinking or confusing himself with thoughts. But every here and there when he was in public, he would survey everybody's tattoos to see if they had circuit designs. He was a hard worker. He liked completing tasks and seeing them through. How do you teach him to let something go? How do you teach him to relax? The strongest part of him is also the weakest. Sometimes, he would drown himself in thought about this case. Things would start to play with his mind; he would imagine things that aren't there. He once followed a person leaving Walgreens that had a circuit board butterfly tattooed on her forearm. He followed her until he retrieved the license plate to her car to do background checks on her on 9 p.m. at night. What Mike said was true. He was being careless with his power, abusive. Leo would suddenly find the discipline to stop. What do you do with that kind of talent, that kind of energy? You put it to work in your favor.

One day, Leo received a phone call from the Amarillo Texas Police Department. They had two guys in custody and both had robot circuit tattoos. They were truckers from Los Angeles to Chicago who were given away by a simple brake lamp that's not working. They decided to bring out the K9s and they found a 5 kg package of cocaine, relatively small amount for a 48 feet trailer but worth detaining nonetheless. When they were being processed, it's when the tattoos were noticed, then due to various agencies working together, Leo Cortez was notified. It was early Friday afternoon when Leo was notified. He decided he would jump in his car, question the individuals personally, and estimate that he would be there by Saturday. He drove all the way there. Leo made it, got in kind of late, and overslept, but they were waiting for him slightly after lunch. That brought the defendants out one at a time and Leo asked them some questions. Leo began by asking the person in custody if it was okay and if he understood that he was just going to ask him some questions. He stated more than likely, nothing said will be used to help nor prosecute his case. The man agreed. Leo started with the basic questions what his name was. What was the name of the person who was with him? What was their relationship? How long had he been a truck driver? Was he legal to work in the United States? They were both Middle Eastern men aged between their mid to late 30s, both immigrants from Turkey, they lived in Bakersfield California, and only the first one was a truck driver. It was the first time he had driven outside of California and his friend wanted to come along. The first guy Leo would question was named Ali Bina, a very clean guy without a criminal history, divorced five years ago, no traffic tickets—nothing whatsoever. He waived the right to have an attorney present because he claimed to be completely innocent and had no problem being asked questions. Leo asked, "What's up with the robot tattoos?" Ali started, "A few years ago, I was beaten up outside a bar badly. These guys just picked on me for no reason. Once I finally get out of hospital, my friend invites me for a drink. I tell him no, I'm never going drinking or to that bar again. After much begging, bringing up old favors and negotiations, my friend Victor talked me into going. When we get there, the same pickup belonging to guys that beat me up with was there. Took a lot of guts to go in. We went inside. All the guys who beat me up were there, but something was different about their appearance. They all have bruises on their face. They see me standing there. They all stand up and walk toward me then say that they are sorry for having humiliated and beaten me. They hand me a jar full of money and told me that my powerful friend saw everything and took care of it. They hung their heads and left. Inside the jar, I find a note. It says, 'Wherever there are circuits, I am there signed the Toolmaker.' Me and my friend start looking at people in the bar and ask them if they are the Toolmaker. None of them are. Some accuse me of being an instigator, provoking fights. It isn't true. Some of the people there had this cool electric circuit tattoo in various designs. They treated us nice, so me and my friend Victor get electric circuit tattoos." Leo was a bit moved, then asked, "And the drugs, how'd you get them?" Ali looked upward then said, "Sir, I know nothing about drugs. All I know is what the log says is in the trailer." He looked panicked or disturbed. May very well be telling the truth as he didn't look like the kind of guy that could win a hand of poker if he had a straight flush. Besides, the doors get tags that cannot be broken in travel unless by law enforcement or where the trailer was sealed when loaded. The only other persons who could know about where it was going were the people who put the drugs in the trailer. A sting is out of the question. The truck is already twenty hours behind schedule and no doubt, there may have been spotters trailing the truck. What a clumsy gamble not fixing the brake lamp unless they wanted the truck to be detained or maybe used as a decoy. Or was the point of it for me to hear Ali Bina's testimony and lay off the case? Take the matter lightly—kind of a check and balances system that protects the righteous and punishes misbehaving people. That seems like an honorable cause, almost as humble as the pay-it-forward idea a while back, but no! This system took the legal system in their own hands acting as a judge, jury, and executioner. Involved in murder and drug trafficking and tempting the weak to fall even deeper into their favorite vice, the thought the FBI are involved boiled Leo's blood. Now, he had to know the truth and was ready to arrest or defraud anyone involved. Leo decided to seek another angle, so he asked, "What was it like when you were arrested? Did anyone follow you? How did the officers who were first on the scene react?" He looked confused. "What do you mean?" Leo turned and looked at the one-way glass as if to imply a conspiracy to see if Ali believed in it, so he asked, "Did the first officers on the scene search the cab or go directly to the trailer? How long after the initial stop did the K-9 unit arrive?" He had a blank stare. It might've been crossing his mind at that moment for the very first time that he may have been set up as part of a conspiracy. Leo said, "What do you think?" Then Ali said, "I have never been pulled over, but I would say the officers were professional and did everything they had to do to ensure everyone's safety." Leo asked, "Did you see any law enforcement officers with robot tattoos?" A guard knocked on the door and yelled, "Times up." Ali had a look of confusion over what Leo had given him. What else was going on in that man's head? Who knows. Ali was removed from the room, then Victor was brought in. He once again went through all the basic questions, then Leo stated, "The reason I am here is because there are similarities between your case and the one I have been assigned to. Let's start by events leading up to the arrest yesterday. What happened?" Victor began, "We woke up in New Mexico, ate breakfast at a truck stop, entered Texas, and everything is fine. We were driving through Amarillo, then I noticed police around our truck, like pacing us, then two SUVs stayed and pulled us over on the outskirts of town. I got handcuffed right away and they separated us. They put me in the trailing SUV. Ali showed them the paperwork. Ali admitted to me that a week ago, he had it in a truck repair shop from the same guy he's been using for years. Me, I didn't like that mechanic. He warned him the wires to the trailer brake lamp bulb were faulty and needed to be replaced. Ali didn't approve of that mechanic's work because when we checked it out, they worked. So, Ali really thought that mechanic was trying to screw us and disliked him even more. On our way entering the state of Texas, we would hear guys on the HAM radio as we passed, mentioning our trailer brake light being out, but Ali didn't believe them." Leo had a half smile. "So, the cops were cool." He was very cool and calmly replied, "Oh yeah, they acted very professional. I was shocked when they put Ali in handcuffs, then one of the officers told me they found drugs inside. I couldn't believe it." Leo made a hand gesture as if to say, go on. "They brought us here to be booked. I mean, I know we're innocent, man. We don't even joke around about that kind of stuff." Leo looked at his file. Victor had been arrested multiple times as a youth in Los Angeles but since he moved to Bakersfield about ten years ago, he's been clean. Leo asked him another question, "What do you do for money, Victor?" He replied,

"I'm a manager at my uncle's convenience store, 2nd and 3rd shift sometimes." Leo carried on, "What's that pay?" Victor said, "Like $400 a week." Leo asked, "Ever been robbed?" Victor responded, "Once or twice." Leo took a gamble to see what Victor's response would be, "They ever propose to you a deal? Protection? What about business? Like deliver items for them?" Victor knew what Leo meant and quickly responded, "No, Sir, never, I fucked up a lot when I was young and learned my lesson. That's it!" Leo asked, "Do you have an electrical circuit design tattoo?" Victor responded, "Yup." He rolled up his right sleeve then showed a picture of two dice made from electric schematic symbols. He also had a name Aaron in electric text on his arm. Leo asked, "Whose Aaron?" Victor replied, "That's my son. His mom left LA and moved to Phoenix. We never married. He's a freshman in high school now." Leo asked, "Why did you get a circuit tattoo?" Victor went blank then said, "Just felt right. Something honest and fair, my vice is gambling so I feel disciplined with it, like I have help to keep me from overdoing it. Look, I might not make a lot of money, but I live well, I save and can afford stuff. I don't need to be smuggling drugs or go-getting Ali in trouble. I love that guy. We live right across the hall from one another." Leo asked, "Are there more people with this tattoo? Is it common?" Victor did a silly little laugh then replied, "Man, everyone I know has tattoos." Leo specified, "With the circuit design?" Victor replied, "They are popular, but some people go too far—" Leo interrupted, "Like what?" Victor said, "Like a cult. I've heard people will follow this guy Toolmaker like he's a God or something." Leo asked, "So you know who he is?" Victor was nodding no then said, "Man, it's got to be a lie. No one can be everywhere and manipulate people like that." Leo asked, "Like a ghost? Is this fairy tale? Urban legend?" Victor answered, "No, most people who wear this are not crazy or troublemakers. They are good, humble, righteous, money-making, happy people." Leo asked, "Do you think organized crime is involved?" Victor smirked then said, "Now hold up, man, hold up, this is not Al Capone or Bugsy Segal. Robots are the future. This feels like hope, like promise, crime does go on, just blame it on a few bad apples. This is something different. I'm telling you, man, it's safe and helps you out." Leo asked, "Do you think the government is involved?" Victor was puzzled then answered, "Maybe, I say this show once about the cold war. They could see and follow people from planes hundreds of miles above us and that was fifty years ago. Nowadays, these satellites can capture images through walls and infrared. They probably shoot lasers into your mind to aggravate you, hear your thoughts, and maybe even hear your voice from outer space." Leo commented, "You're a sci-fi fan, aren't you? Well, if they could track everyone's movements all the time, I wouldn't be here. I'd be back in Houston getting ready for my date because we would backtrack the 5 kilograms of drugs all the way back to the opium farm and arrest everyone involved." Victor grew some sense of religion and said, "History has taught us that when in good graces, even murder is allowed. What if our God is greater than their god? What if there was a neutralizer? What if this Toolmaker really exists? What if maybe he's watching us right now? What would you ask him for, Special Agent Cortez?" Leo shrugged his shoulders then answered, "How about a decent cup of coffee?" Just then, two guards entered the room and said, "Times up." They escorted Victor out of the room. Unknowingly behind the one-way glass, another police officer found Leo's comment about asking for decent coffee humorous. Leo tried to get another question in and asked, "How do I find this group? What do they call themselves?" Victor was already out of the room, but he heard the question and began shouting the answer. "Oh, don't worry, they'll find you, maybe they already have."

One of the officers who was chaperoning Leo poked his head in the doorway then said, "Detective Spencer is on his way. . . geez, that guy is nuts, huh." Leo threw his hand up as if to say he doesn't know. The seed of doubt had been laid in Leo's mind. He stopped the recording and began taking down the names of officers who were on site now and listing all arresting officers. Leo requested to stay in the interrogation room for as long as it took Detective Spencer to arrive, the room was not needed. Permission was then granted. Once the detective arrived, he knocked then entered. "Hey, how's it going? You must be Leo Cortez. Edward Spencer here with the Amarillo PD. Sorry I'm late, coffee?" Spencer was carrying two freshly brewed cups from Dunkin Donuts, which is Leo's favorite. "Yeah, sure how did you know?" Leo reached over and took a cup. Spencer looked like a camp scout leader. The guy had probably never set foot in a bar. He had the biggest set of glasses Leo has ever seen but he got the coffee right, so Leo thought highly of him already. He thought he might as well pick his mind. Leo asked him, "What do you think of the two guys we have here?" Spencer sat back and answered, "Well, to me, it looks pretty cut and dry. These two guys were being threatened back home to drive that load across the country, but our guys got them. Good old keen eye police work. I-40 is used by these smugglers constantly. It's one of their best routes. We do the best we can watching that strip." Leo asked, "You don't believe they are operating alone?" Spencer replied, "Highly unlikely although it's not a lot. I don't think these guys would've had enough money to make that kind of purchase and engineer a trip. It's the carelessness to have a brake lamp out their operation. Everything would be accounted for. These two guys probably got pushed into it or just plain and simply didn't know about it. Up to the judge." Spencer gave some very solid answers. I guess the scout did know a thing or two. "What's your next move, Mr. Cortez?" Leo replied, "Backtrack every stop that the truck made. Look at surveillance footage to see if the rear was tampered with by anyone. All the way back to California if necessary." Spencer said, "Good luck." Leo replied, "Sure. Thanks for the coffee." Leo gathered his equipment and his files and began to make his way out of the building. An officer escorted him right outside the door in the hallway and walked them through all of the checkpoints out to the parking garage. Once Leo got into his vehicle, he checked his phone. He had a missed phone call and a voicemail from the girl he was supposed to go out and have dinner with tonight. It looks like dinner was cancelled and that was how he spent the rest of his night—backtracking surveillance footage GPS notations and looking at highway cameras for any suspicious patterns.

CHAPTER 7

Leo did not find anything suspicious on the semi-truck after watching a video en route to Amarillo but the surveillance cameras for the warehouse where it was last loaded did not have all its cameras online that day. California it is. Leo had already been two days away from his home. He was not eating well and all he could think about was this one case that he continued unravelling but was not even close to making an arrest. He began overthinking and doubt crept in. Leo completed background checks and kept tabs on the members of Amarillo PD who were involved in Ali's and Victor's arrest. However, nothing came back on them as being negative or incriminating. They were clean. He spent time thinking of possible moles in the bureau where he worked but truthfully, he didn't know anyone long enough to draw that kind of conclusion. He was losing track of time and never called his date back. His priorities were set. This case had enough on it to continue pursuing and made an attempt to finalize. During that long drive west, he began doubting his own role in all this. Was someone watching his every move? Was he the mole and didn't know it? Was this his vice? Is this his downfall? Curiosity. He just wasn't the type of guy to let it go. He felt as if he was onto something big—something that could change lives. Is there a guy who calls himself Toolmaker? If he does so much good for people, then why traffic drugs? Why murder? And who knows what else he's into? He meant to find out. He checked into a small motel in the San Bernardino Valley. It was late Sunday. Leo decided to treat himself to a steak dinner, then after watching a bit of sports channel, dozed off and got some much-needed rest. Monday at about 9:30 a.m., his boss called him on his cellphone, wanting to be filled in on the details of Leo's investigation. Leo tried to make it seem like he was on the edge of making an arrest, exaggerating the case like he was close to closing it. His boss didn't buy it but wouldn't shut him down because he was still relatively new there in Houston. His boss wanted to show a vow of confidence in Leo's work and said, "Follow your leads until Friday. If you come up empty on Saturday, I need you off this case! Understood?" Leo agreed, "Yes, sir." I guess he needed to hear that and to be held again to the fact that this was no vacation. He needed to focus on results. He went to that warehouse, the last place the trailer that Ali Bina was hauling with his semi-truck had last been open. Leo approached the office, identified himself, and explained the situation. They were very helpful and compliant in everything Leo asked for. The company did have a footage of the inside of the warehouse on VHS. Leo was able to single out an outside employee who sneaked in and placed the box inside the trailer when no one was looking. How did he know the destination or the time the trailer would be loaded? Who else had access to that information? All the logs that are posted by the shipping bays and container numbers are assigned to different people. Leo conducted a series of random interrogations to all twenty-five employees but resulted in nothing concrete. Nobody knew anything. The suspect just walks in as if from the shadows and the image is too distorted even after analyzed by a local video film specialist. There was not enough to go off to make any accusations by appearance. Leo was mentally drained, tired, and exhausted himself. It was now late Tuesday and he had nothing but a blurry VHS tape. Leo was frustrated. He got some drive thru food, checked into a motel, and fell asleep.

The following day, he woke up in a good mood, felt rejuvenated, went on a jog, went over to a local diner, and had a nice breakfast. Deciding to go over the simple things and see what comes up, he grabbed a notebook and reviewed what he knew and what he wanted to know. Leo listed the things he had done and tried and things he can still try and what was next. After some time, he concluded to lure out the robot circuit gang by looking as they do, seeing if he could get invited into the brethren. It would have to look good and convincing. He went by a local art school and searched the bulletin board looking for an artist who does tattoos, although Leo wanted something temporary that looked real. His level of commitment still had a ceiling (maybe that's why he wasn't making any arrests). He found one that had an attractive-looking ad, looking like they put some time into it, so Leo called him and explained what he wanted. The artist agreed to work in inks and markers advising that after about a week, it should be gone. Once Leo arrived, the artist claimed to have an emergency to attend to and not be able to work on Leo that afternoon, so Leo offered him more money but it was to no use. Down the street was a spooky-looking tattoo parlor in the second floor of a laundromat. Leo went inside and explained what he wanted. The artist declined unless he could perform with his unique natural ink pigments, which is of course, permanent. Leo accepted. So, Leo spent that afternoon getting his own robot circuits tattoo. He picked an outlined metal skeleton frame on the backside of his right hand. It looked awesome. Next, he drove to Bakersfield, the same bar where Ali and Victor had had their encounter. Leo wanted to draw attention to see if anyone confronted or restrained him. He was acting like a fool, betting on pool, trying to start betting poker matches, flirting with the waitresses, and yes, his right hand in plain view so that everybody could see he was in with the circuit crew. He spent the next two nights in that bar or in a few nearby, but with no luck. Just like hanging a cross around your neck doesn't make you Catholic, having designs on your skin doesn't get you in. It was now Friday. Leo was angry with himself. His plan had not worked, so he had to face the music. He couldn't crack this nut. It was beyond him; he was already defeated. On this night, he went to the bar to do what most people go to a bar for—get a beer and watch the game. It was a busy night. There were a lot of people. He was feeling sad, lonely, and depressed thinking he couldn't do something he had trained to do. His attempts meant nothing at this point. It didn't even matter what it was he was doing wrong. In his mind, he was already driving East to Houston. Then a woman approached him. "Do you want to play poker?" she asked in a very soft, inviting voice. He didn't even turn to look at her. The Lakers were losing to the Bulls going into the fourth quarter. "New, I didn't bring my deck," he said. "That's alright. You can use mine. I'm Esmeralda." Now he turned and was feeling lucky again and said, "Leo, What'll you drink?" She had already taken the chair next to him and said, "Heineken." He nodded his approval, then signaled to the bartender who caught his gesture and shortly brought it over. Esmeralda said, "You know, I saw you in here a few days ago and something was off about you. Just didn't seem right." Leo faced her and said, "Oh that I'm from out of town?" She pointed skyward with her index finger while holding her beer with the same hand, then said, "Hmm, maybe, but you know, people who usually have that kind of tattoo are well-kept, dressed clean, are happy, don't gamble, or take chances like you. You're trying to get yourself arrested." She was smiling, he through his eyebrows upward then claimed, "You're telling me I'm dirty, miserable, and fat! Wow." They both broke out laughing. Now Leo was in his mid to late twenties, a handsome-looking guy with a nice frame but the fact was he hadn't been taking care of himself on this trip—eating junk food at all random times, got a flabby look lately, and didn't really pack for a week's worth of staying away from home. He did some shopping in Tuesday at a Walmart, got some jeans, a t-shirt, and some sweats to sleep in. He was wearing a suit when he met up with Ali and Victor. It had been used a couple of times and it was currently at the cleaners. Yet, despite all that she saw, she took a chance on him. What a girl, he smiled, then said, "Alright, you win. I've been down lately, haven't been showing my body the respect it deserves." She looked at Leo's hand, the one with the new ink on, and examined it. He said, "What?" She looked up and said, "Do you know what this is? It's a reminder to love yourself all the way to the bone." Leo looked puzzled. "How so?" She smiled then said, "Well, look, I have a small robot canary on my wrist because it was canary's song I used to sing when I was younger, and I loved it a lot. I was the front singer on a rock band. My boyfriend hated it. I thought that he was a man. He was being protective and caring about me. He was just enacting his own jealousy. The worst part was when I stopped singing, everything got worst. I finally broke up with him, then a friend asked me to get a robot tattoo because robots have no attachment. They can let things go and be new to someone else. So, I did it." Leo nodded to show he was still listening. The part where she mentioned her ex was just not very pleasing for him to hear. Esmeralda noticed, so she was searching for a way to wrap it up, then said, "I asked God for help one night, for strength to stay away from him. A few days later, I saw an ad to sing on a band again. I tried out and got it. I get to travel a lot and do back up for famous singers. It's awesome. I love it. The best part is I've never seen him again." Leo couldn't believe his luck on the last night in town. He met an amazing woman. He was not a fan of the long-distance thing and her c'mon-what-are-the-chances attitude of approaching him. They spent the next thirty minutes enjoying each other's company, then Leo noticed he was being watched by multiple people around the bar.

As he attempted to indiscreetly identify any key features from any of them, one guy immediately caught his attention. It was his best friend from his old neighborhood, BertDog. Leo had no hesitation to call him over to join him. What were the odds? Maybe Leo was losing focus and his personal human element was deceiving his common sense, but in his mind, he had already given up on the case. This was fun time. With a big smile on both their faces, they shook hands and gave each other a hug. Esmeralda got up and removed herself. Probably thinking she had misjudged Leo, she said, "I'll let you two catch up. I'll be over there. Nice meeting you." And just like that, she was gone. Leo could not see the road moving in front of him. This was too big of a coincidence. Decisions come and go, each determining what happens next. The glory of it is you can't go back. Leo told BertDog, "Hey, man, how you been?" BertDog replied, "Funny because just a week ago, I was paying commissary to get Twinkies upstate, wasn't due for parole for two more years, then they call me and say I'll be out Tuesday and if I wanted to join a work program right here in South Cal. I said *hell yeah* and here I am. What about you?" All the sudden, Leo remembered he was an FBI agent. This work stresses people in that manner, making them forget how to relax. Leo did not want to use his friend or lie to him, then he noticed the set of random coincidences. He thought this might be the break his investigation needed, so Leo simply said, "You know, picking up girls." They turned and looked. There was already another guy trying to talk with Esmeralda. BertDog said chuckling, "Looks like you struck out. You still don't know anything about woman, do you? They like to be loved, attention, detail. C'mon man, I read the Carma Sutra. I had to. All the pictures were torn off, only thing left was the text. Am I going to have to teach you everything like when we were kids?" They both had a good laugh. They were catching up and having a lot of laughs, but Leo thought he would try his old friend. Maybe the case was not lost yet. Bert was asking Leo, "Word around the street was that you took that gun Kilo's cousin gave you when we were kids and held up the convenience store. The clerk and a customer got shot. Everyone blamed it on you, then you disappeared. We all heard you were serving time. All four of those other guys got caught. Everyone knew who they were. I saw Kilo once during court and he said you were supposed to give him the signal. It was clear, but there were witnesses in there and they shot them. Heck. I swear you were in the cell next to mine once, but they transferred you before I could see you." Leo had seen the report, and nowhere did it mention a Leonardo Cortez, although he does remember that day especially the break he received from that detective the following day. Luckily, BertDog couldn't tell the difference and he went on, "Yeah, they must've thrown you up here in Cali. They got bigger prisons." Leo took another drink then asked, "What happened to the four of them?" Bert got really close. "Oh, don't worry about them. They all lied and threw you under the bus, claimed that you were the mastermind, that you threatened them, and that you did the robbing and the shooting yourself, then cleared the register because the only thing they got was 14 dollars and 25 cents. Man, they named every person whoever knew you. They even planned to have people on the outside go and your intimate family just because they were pissed at you, even me. Before that order was carried out, the guys carrying out the hit died—blasted by automatic gunfire. Bro, you became my hero. Everyone backed off what with you making hits even when in prison, having their own guys rat each other out. Damn. Baby was the weakest of the four. The other three assumed he leaked info on the hit to you, especially because he was cousin with that one girl you liked. One day just a month in, they smashed his face with a barbell. But the guy running the yard was this big black dude named Money, and they fucked up. They didn't ask Money for permission to take care of Baby even if he was their own. They planned to jump him, but Money has been through that game a bunch of times and saw them coming. Money waited until they went for it but the whole cell block was on his side. They helped Money, and Kilo and 8Ball died. Joker was the baldest of them all, had some good connections and young guys that well, used to look up to him. Joker was in the hospital for weeks. I heard Money put his foot up Joker's butt. Well, maybe just the big toe. He pleaded out on condition to be transferred out of state." They both grimaced a little. Leo asked, "What about you, what'd you do? You were like a money-making genius." Bert liked the comment then started, "Man, the block was hot. People were getting arrested and shot. I left to San Antonio but you can't take the ghetto out of the man. It was a fresh untapped territory. I was attending community college but the real reason I was there was to sell dope and it flew out the trunk of my Honda. Man, one night I was partying, and I crashed my car all drunk and blown out my mind. There was a trooper about two cars back and saw the whole thing. I had about 500 grams of coke in my trunk. I was able to convince them it was personal use, but they still gave me ten years." Leo had a shocked look on his face then said, "Whoa, man, that sucks, so have you had any yet?" Bert smiled, "Actually my PO just made me go take a drop today. I just scored some from those guys over there. You in?" Leo wanted to talk him out of it but was worried he might blow his cover. "Naw." BertDog caught a good look at Leo's new tattoo. "Hey, you roll with those robot guys now?" Pointing at his hands, Leo replied, "Kind of." BertDog was nodding up and down in approval and said, "I heard of a club in LA where they party till 6 in the morning. You down?" Leo's big break? Leo said, "Okay, let's go." He paid the bartender then they walked on out. They were going in Leo's car. He scrambled to cover the files and anything that might make him look weird. BertDog noticed some files and notebooks and said, "You're a student?" Leo replied, "Yeah I do some studying. Sometimes."

CHAPTER 8

The place was in a popular part of town with a very good night life atmosphere. The building was huge. There were people everywhere. However, it wasn't until they finally got to the door that he caught the name Lasor's. The tattoo paid off. They were in. BertDog had already taken his bump. Leo was asked if he wanted to go to the party upstairs. They agreed and started to make their way. There was a second-floor party, which is maybe for members only. The crowd got cleaner, the music was trendier, and the staff was more formal, even elegant. To get to the stairs, you had to cross the entire main level dance floor which was very crowded. It was hard to walk, then Leo had to show his tattoo to the bouncers at the entrance to a stairway that went upstairs. Once upstairs, there were other lines but more casual and relaxed. There were face painting booths and airbrushing going on in the hallway, then there was a second cover. They were charged before they went inside. I guess, they weren't that exclusive to the club yet. Leo and BertDog declined any paint and once inside, they were amazed at the sort of club they saw—the most amazing and extravagant group of party-goers they had ever seen partying. The room was full of good-looking people having a good time, and needless to say, the theme was robot circuit tattoo or glow in the dark painted on designs, but the coolest part was a grid of black light hanging only at about 8 feet off the ground. When people walked beneath it, their faces lit up in black light paint in various designs similar to Marvel's Ironman helmet among other robot designs. It was very cool. Even people who seemed like geeks or nerds were jumping and having a good time alongside girls that looked like million-dollar models. There were no labels and no differences in there. Everybody was just having fun expressing the human part in them but looking like robots. They stood there for about fifteen minutes just watching the rest of the world having fun. The DJ was wearing an oversized Futurama Bender head, mixing tracks brilliantly. It was just the place to be. Suddenly, a Hispanic guy who he himself could have been a model came up to Leo and threw his arm over Leo's neck then talked to him close to his ear as it was loud in there. He said, "Right now, there are three things you can be—a cop, a snitch, or a party-goer." Leo wrestled to get a grip on his rest, ready to toss him across the floor, then the guy said, "Whoa, whoa, whoa, take it easy. I'm on your side. I'm LAPD. We are both working on the same case. I'm on the trail for Toolmaker too. I'm going to pull something out of my pocket. I want you to turn around and sniff it." Leo looked at him in complete anger. Just before Leo got a chance to throw a fit, the guy said, "Look, everybody here knows me but they don't know you. In about five minutes, if you keep this funeral look, you're going to get it kicked out of you. You flash that badge, you're done! Back to Texas in a body bag." Leo looked around and sure enough, a few very large guys were looking right at him, so he turned around and cleared a small amount of coke. This guy, he just laced the back of Leo's left hand. The party kept going. "No willpower? You're desperate for an arrest, aren't you?" He was smiling. Leo wanted to punch the guy but then submitted to his scheme. Leo asked him, "Who are you?" The guy answered, "Anthony Carrillo. Detective. I just saved your life. I've been trying to bring down Toolmaker for years. Your boss called me and asked me to help you. This is *my* town." Leo asked, "What do you have?" Leo pulled Anthony away from BertDog to not blow his cover. BertDog was not exactly focused at the time. Anthony began telling Leo, "I have reason to believe Toolmaker is in town. He has been supplying half the country from here in Los Angeles with weapons and drugs, people trafficking and overseeing all crime and theft going by the name El General." Leo was starting to feel the effects of the drugs he took. The stuff Anthony was saying was vague, so he was processing the information slower and replied, "What. That's not the guy. The guy we're looking for comes on as a savior doing good and holding people responsible for their own actions by their own hand." Anthony busted out laughing, "Savior? This guy is evil and elusive You must mean *el diablo*? C'mon, that's make-believe—saving people. Next, you're going to tell me Toolmaker can read your thoughts. All hocus pocus." Leo's eyes were glaring. "He can do that?" Anthony said, "No, silly. Hey, there goes Tina and Maricruz. C'mon buddy."

They hadn't noticed but BertDog had wandered into the bathroom. Some guys followed him into bathroom and one of them who was quickest with the tongue said, "Hey man, need a bump?" BertDog said, "No thanks, I still got some." The cholo-looking guy said, "Oh, alright cool, my name is Gordo, yo. Don't I know you from somewhere?" Gordo must've been one of those oxymoron things because the guy was long and skinny. BertDog said, "You ever do time in Texas?" The guy answered, "No," but then their conversation went on that soon, they were talking like lifelong friends. It went on for a few more minutes, then the guy said, "So who's your friend?" referring to Leo. Bert answered, "Oh, that's my boy Leo. We go way back." Gordo nodded in agreement up and down as if to say yes, then he asked another question, "Did he do time in Texas too?" Bert went off what he knew beforehand. Leo had yet to entirely tell him anything of his current dealings, so he said, "Oh yeah, he robbed a store and shot two people when he was seventeen. He's done a lot of time." Gordo and the guys looked shocked and he pointed with his thumb toward the direction of the bathroom exit. "That dude? Well, how'd he get out of it?" Bert's bump was wearing off so when he spoke next, he was messing with his eye movement as if to regain focus, then he said, "This OG took the wrap for him." All their jaws fell to the floor. Who was this guy and why was he so important? A few of them in the back started talking amongst themselves saying, "I bet he's the Toolmaker, homies." Then some were whispering. Even the people who were using the urinals stopped and turned their heads to see who the Toolmaker keeps as company. "Yeah, he was coming to town." Bert was still nodding up and down, then the guy asked him, "Oh yeah, and what was he and the cop talking about?" BertDog was getting ready to head on out. "I don't know. I think the other guy called him Toolmaker." There were six guys in total who were part of El General's crew making some rounds supplying and collecting money. Just the right place at the right time couldn't have picked a better person to ask but Bert. Bert left the bathroom and made his way over to Leo and Anthony. The guy he was with in the bathroom went and gave Leo a final look, then Gordo decided to call his boss although it was late. His boss did not like to be disturbed afterhours, but he made the call. His boss, El General, answered in a bad mood as he was watching a movie with his wife and daughter in his Santa Barbara beachside home. "What is it?" he exclaimed. The guy on the line was a faithful and strong type of guy. Gordo said, "General, I think we just ran into the Toolmaker." El General didn't really believe such a person even existed, much less that he could beat him at his own game in his hometown, so he ordered, "Well, what are you doing? Get the men you need, kick his ass, and bring him to me!" The guy on the other end looked confident but had to issue a disclaimer, "We're at Lasor's. There are like two thousand of his people in here." El General said, "Ah, are you sure it's him?" Gordo exclaimed, "This guy has a past. People take his falls. He beats the court system and rubs elbows with police. Does blow in the open." El General started worrying a bit then he said, "What does he look like?" Gordo said, "He doesn't look vicious, but yeah, pretty boy, MMA stance, Mexican. This boy is from Texas. He's got this dude that's known him for a long time, says they're friends and that they both have done time in Texas. *Pa mi,* it's him, man, Toolmaker, but moving on, him in here would be suicide. We need more men to take him down!" El General was flipping through some notes, "Is Carrillo there?" The guy answered, "Sir, they're sitting together." El General mumbled to himself, "That rotten two-faced pig." Then he commands, "Not tonight. So, he knows Carrillo, bad move. Take a picture of the Toolmaker and his friends. We'll lay low for now so they won't see it coming." Gordo was excited to hear his orders and said, "Simon General." Now Leo had no clue of all the activity going on around him. All he could think about was the pretty Hispanic girl sitting next to him and his new friend Anthony pouring liquor into his glass. From brief conversation, it sounded like everyone knew Anthony was a cop, and everyone knew he did drugs, sold them, and stole them from guys who were not cooperating with El General. He bragged of high profile arrests he made against some very dangerous drug dealers. He even showed the girls his tattoo from his days as a marine, then one of the girls asked, "Were you in Afghanistan?" He answered, "I served before the US went in but later, went over privately." The girls were in awe. "A professional." He had this very arrogant look and even gave a top-heavy nod like we were on some country club golf range, then he said, "Well, you know." The girls were eating it up then one of them asked, "How many people did you kill? Did you make a lot of money?" Before Carrillo could answer, the other girl asked, "Ooh, did you steal Arabian gold?" He was all smiles. "Ladies, a friend of mine is a Security Private Contractor who landed a job with the government. He needed some more guys. The pay was great, and we went over there and *regulated*!" He said that very loudly and pronounced that they had a lot of laugh. Then, Bert who had joined them reasked a question from one of the girls but he asked a lot more seriously, "*Yeah*! So, how many people did you kill?" Carrillo got serious too then he said, "None. It's not Hollywood over there. It's regular people who might not want us there. We had methods of getting information that the military couldn't succumb to, then pass that intel along. However, I did make some very solid connections and some great friends over there." Carrillo gave Bert a deep stare as if to say "none of your business," then Carrillo looked over to the girls and hugged them both saying, "And keep making new friends every single day, like you beautiful girls." They all laughed. He reached over and kissed Maricruz. The guy lacked *no* confidence. Anthony was what Leo thought of when they say keep it a hundred. This was keeping it real—believing in yourself, enjoying life, aiming for something, then going after it. This guy was instantly Leo's role model. Carrillo noticed the Ocho's who were with Bert in the bathroom then pointed it out to Leo. Leo was tripping very bad. Thankfully, he was sitting down. Carrillo simply said, "I'll fill you in another day." The guys from the bathroom were known as the Eighty Ninth Ocho's and yes, there were Eighty Ninth Nueve's, but those were on the east part of the street. The Ocho's were on the west both under control by guys loyal to El General. Carrillo kept track of their position even though they had split up to keep a watchful eye on their suspected Toolmaker. It turned into a long night. As it turned to 1:30 a.m., the ladies felt comfortable enough to leave with these guys and keep the party going. BertDog had to go use the bathroom. He got up and moved away from the table, so once again, Gordo followed him in and signaled to the other Eighty Ninth Ocho's to keep an eye on their suspect. He again approached BertDog. "Hey carnal, what's happening?" BertDog was done drying his hands and shook Gordo's hand like they were good friends, then Gordo said, "Struck out? Got a girl? Here, man, let me hook you up, c'mon." He went outside and walked up to a drunk girl who was nearly asleep in a chair. He whispered something in her ear. She looked at BertDog and just like that, she was ready to leave with him. She then got up and wrapped her arm around Bert's. Gordo said, "See, man, I take care of mine, but hey, let me get your number. You can get mine. I can get you anything." As he said that, he was taping on his nose. BertDog caught on and they both laughed. BertDog replied, "Thanks, bro, but all this seems a little fishy. I'm good." I guess Bert had some sense left in him after all. "I use a guy who I did time with. The girl, it'd be nice, but she's drunk, man, I can't do it. Sorry, bro, I don't roll like that." Gordo reached and grabbed BertDog by the arm as he started to walk away, then said, "Tell you what, I got a single shot right here on the house. I won't bother you but I don't answer calls from people I don't know. Let me get your number so, *andale*." BertDog's willpower suffered a moment of weakness. He took the tiny blue bag with a key tip amount of cocaine inside of it. They exchanged phone numbers and Bert went back. They were getting ready to leave. Everybody there knew Anthony. He tipped the waitress who flirted with him. As he walked by the bartenders, he shook hands, and tipped everyone. The lead bartender, an Asian girl who looked very athletic with a huge amount of attitude toward him, was the only one who refused his money. Then, as they walked out, everybody addressed him as Mister Carrillo. Leo was coming around feeling better. He noticed he had not seen any robot circuit tattoos on Anthony. How did he get in? Who was this guy? Each of them was going separate ways, but before that, Anthony went into the bathroom, so Leo took advantage of this opportunity and asked Tina, "Can I have a word with Maricruz really quick?" She said, "Yeah." Leo walked over next to her waiting on Anthony, tapped her arm gently, and said, "Hey, ugh, I made a bet with a friend as to how many tattoos Anthony has. If by chance you see him naked tonight, can you check to see how many tattoos he has? Let me know what they look like. Please" She looked at him like she was going to slap Leo for insinuating anything, then she saw an angle and replied, "$100." Leo said, "Good, so $50 right now, and $50 when you tell me?" She looked uninterested, turned in a different direction, then Maricruz said, "Yeah that's fine." Leo said, "Okay, Tina can give you the remainder, but I need to know." Leo reached in his wallet and handed her $50. She said, "Sure." Anthony came out of the bathroom. He had texted the valet downstairs to bring his car upfront. When they finally made their way outside, there was Anthony's car 20 feet from the door. Anthony tipped the valet who replied, "Keys are inside, Sir. Have a good night" hinting toward the sporty coupe, a BMW M3 customed out with big shiny wheels and that trendy (back in the mid to late 2000s) Comillian Purple Pearl color. Maricruz got inside. Leo and Tina were giggling, then Leo announced, "Ugh, we're taking a cab." BertDog wanted to drive Leo's car to the hotel his work had assigned for him, although Leo said he couldn't let him drive his car because he had important papers in there. BertDog pushed and Leo gave in, but he said, "Don't look at anything and call me around noon so you can pick me up." BertDog said, "No problem." Anthony revved the car up, rolled down the window, and yelled, "We got to meet tomorrow too, business. Okay?" Leo yelled toward him as he was entering a cab, "Okay." There were a lot of people outside, and everywhere, all three cars were being followed by multiple people— all part of El General.

CHAPTER 9

The phone was ringing. It was 10:05 a.m., Saturday. Leo awoke naked in a Marriot Suites near LAX airport. Tina was lying next to him with her partial back facing towards him. Her soft bosom was neatly lying on her chest like circular bags of gelatin with a set of small areolas. At that time, her nipples lay flush. He could see the breaths of air she inhaled by the lifting surges of her body. He answered the phone. It was his boss. "Why are you still in LA?" Leo was rubbing his eyes. "Sir, I've been doing some deep undercover work and I really feel like I've been making progress. We've identified the leader of the robot circuit gang which go by machines, an underworld boss by the name of El General and—" His boss interrupted him, "Hold up. El General is untouchable. Do not pursue! And what is this we? Bullshit." Leo continued by telling him about Carrillo, "Well, Sir, I've met with a local detective by the name of Anthony Carrillo. He's been helping me on the case." His boss was angry and said, "Dammit! *Son* Carrillo is dirty. Do not have any contact with him unless you want to share a cell with him. As for El General, he's off the hooks. Don't awake a giant. His real identity is still unknown to us. Heck. The only known photos we have of him are from the mid-nineties. That town runs deep. There are other investigations going on, but I can't tell you which way to lean or what to do. You're a full-blown agent but giving this case to you was a mistake. I never asked LAPD for support, but I did make a call to the LA Bureau in case you contacted them. Rest assured, they'll be on your butt from now until you leave town." Leo's Boss hung up. Leo stood and washed up. He felt hungover like he was a teenager again with a lack of willpower, just going with the flow. Then, the thought of this case crept in. He felt like he's advancing but then, reality fell in and he was convinced he was just spinning his wheels in the mud burying himself deeper and deeper. Tina awoke. She called Maricruz. As she was on the phone with her, Leo filled in Tina on his supposed bet. He signaled that he wanted to know about Anthony's tattoos. As Maricruz was telling Tina, she was repeating them to Leo, and apparently, he had multiple tattoos. He had a marine eagle on his right arm, squad name on his right forearm, a holy Celtic cross on his shoulder, and names and dates of friends who had died while in service on the right-side ribcage. Then, she said he had airplanes on his left ribcage, like ten of them ranging from Cessna's to commercial airliners. Leo was back in investigator mode. Could he also be the lost son of Amaro Carrillo Fuentes? The gears were turning heavily in Leo's mind. Tina enjoyed their time together, so she went downstairs and just made it in time to get a late breakfast from the hotel serving area. She brought enough for the two of them. They continued with flirtish horseplay, then after a while, Maricruz was downstairs to pick up Tina. Leo gave Tina the money he had promised Maricruz and asked Tina if he could see her again. She gave him her number and said, "Call me?" He agreed. He contacted BertDog and told him to bring some lunch as he was still hungry. BertDog said, "You want a large fry and large drink?" Leo exclaimed, "Hell yeah!" Then, Leo got to working figuring things out. If Carrillo is not a machine, how did he know of FBI investigating? If he wasn't in with the machines, how did he know of the machines in LA? Who could have tipped him off? It didn't seem like El General is friends with him, or are they? What does the LAPD know about the Toolmaker? Did LA make the whole thing up? All the way to Texas? What's the connection? Is it possible Carrillo is *the* Toolmaker and can read minds? *Whoa.* Everyone at the club worshipped him, except for that one girl, but he paid them, so of course, they would be polite. All the money he was throwing around—where does he get his money from? Leo went to work on call with a person in the Houston Bureau assisting him, finding everything he could about Anthony Carrillo. No father listed; only a mother, an Emily Morales of San Bernardino who showed to own multiple properties. Then, he began looking into Anthony's investments—only one property, income stream. He had his cell phone number. They traced his last known location. It was 10 minutes from LAX. It looked like he was on his way to where Leo was. Maricruz may have told him either that or he really can read minds. The fact was that he was unassigned to help Leo. How did he find him? How did he earn his trust? Who really was Anthony Carrillo? Then that very moment, his phone gave off some weird static noise and he lost his phone call. He opened the window then peered out as if to see if someone was interfering with the signal or to see something suspicious. It's indeed something out of the ordinary. While he was observing the scenery, BertDog had pulled up and Leo noticed three other cars pull up behind Bert. Thirteen guys in total came out and made their way to the Ford Taurus. BertDog had just been driving. Another two guys emerged from inside a parking lot garage across the street, totaling fifteen guys. Then, one of them was on the phone for a brief second or two. After hanging up, he went to the trunk of the first car, opened it, then gave instructions by pointing to whatever was inside. Then, everybody reached in and grabbed a gun. There were a wide range of different weapons in that car's trunk ranging from handguns to shotguns and even fully automatic assault rifles. The NRA would've been proud. BertDog was being followed. The two who came from within the parking lot had more than likely been sitting on Leo's location all night. Leo grabbed a small knife, put on a coat, then went down the hall to the elevator. His assigned firearm was locked in the glovebox of his car. His plan was to maneuver around them without being seen and reach his firearm attempting to find a phone and call it in to local authorities. Leo would not get that chance. He went to the stairs and could hear them making their way up. He raced over to the next elevator and pressed the button, but before the doors could open, Leo noticed he was crowded by four very large men. Leo was nervous and started to reach for the knife, then one of the guys said, "I'll take that. Don't worry, the boss wants to talk with you." They escorted Leo out of the building, went into the parking lot garage, and asked him to climb into a covered van. BertDog was already there and it looked like he put up a fight for his face was beaten. Leo was tied up with a duct tape around his hands and one ankle with Bert's and the other to the driver's seat frame. They left and were on the road for about an hour. Then, they put a paper bag over Leo's head and removed him from the back of the van to be escorted inside a building. It was near the water; you could hear seagulls. They had radios and were relaying information over through coded messages. Leo was attempting to decipher the code, but he bluntly heard them say Carrillo got away. Leo was in that room in an old warehouse near the water with twelve guys watching over him for about six hours. They took his bag off and were playing card games right next to where Leo and BertDog were being kept. Their hands were still bound, one ankle with the other guys. The guys brought pizza and gave some to their prisoners. Then, another group of twenty showed up in five cars. One of them was a Lincoln Town car all costumed out and from the back door stepping out was a man who was a shadow in Los Angeles, El General. Leo muttered when he was getting closer to BertDog, "El General." He was close enough to them to have heard and said, "Yes, that is I. Now, the only reason I would take the time to meet with you is that some of my best guys believe you are someone of great importance." He looked disappointed at his associate known as Chino, then El General addressed all the men, "They believe you to be the Toolmaker. However, I have used my resources and found out who you really are, even prepared all that info into a nice little file right here. See." He took a seat and began to flip through a file he had with him. El General said, "You're just a federal agent, not even a good one." BertDog looked over at Leo in shock. El General went on, "I can have you drug tested. I can pin so many crimes on you, your life is over. You think no one saw or recorded what you did or who you were with last night? Do you think you can do whatever you want? I run the West Coast. Everything goes through me from cyber hacking all the way to a Billy stealing a bag of .25 cent Doritos. Machines, hmmm, a bunch of people looking for a way to avoid paying the piper. People are weak. They feel like they need guidance, a new path. They're pathetic, grouping together praying to someone new, this Toolmaker. You, Mister Cortez, are too young and too much of a fool to be the Toolmaker. You have no will, no grapefruits. You see, you have nothing, the way I see it, or you leave this room with a new boss or chopped up into little pieces." Then, Leo firmly said, "I *am* the Toolmaker! I lead the army of the machines. I am everywhere!" The guys were laughing and chuckling, but the tone and amount of confidence in Leo even when faced with death was too much that even El General had to pause and re-evaluate his stance on Leo. Could it really be him? Toolmaker is to El General like an old wives' tale, like an urban legend. The elder narcos he had met while coming up had told him, "The only way to advance is by killing the man above you, then one day, you will not find no man above you, but rest assured, someone is there watching you, waiting for you to *fuck up*!" El General had been cautious, leaving the old neighborhood and promoting people he knew away from that life so that they would never identify him as being involved. He started businesses and donated his time and money for everyone seeking help, but he also heard all the cries of the weak and the desperate seeking vice drugs, gambling, prostitution, trafficking, theft, and online scams. Almost coincidentally, people were willing to make some money on the side working for him. El General thrived in his later years never even having to be in the same room, like the Bureau said, "We weren't even sure what he looked like." From the last picture, he hadn't changed, probably even looking younger and fitter like he does PX90. Previously, he looked more like a neighborhood *cholo*, but now he grew out some hair, got no piercings nor visible tattoos, and still rocked white tennis shoes, which looked so smooth like they just came out the box. He looked like a neat suburban Los Angeles Mexican-American father, possibly grandfather, but there was a key feature that he may carry with him until he dies. That cold and deep (I'm about to kill you and tear your head off with a dull knife) very intimidating look. El General had to be cautious of the people he had under him. If they were paid and remained disciplined, they'd stay. He had a long chain of command beneath him but recently, there's this talk of these machines being a new source for their vice and in *his* town! It was not meant for him to share or compete for prices or turf that he had long since conquered. The machines made all the people El General employed nervous. El General did know about Laredo. He was being provided for from stolen merchandise of his contractors who operate out of Laredo. El General wanted to take the machine's merchandise and their money, and who knows, maybe he could dissolve the machines who until now had not had a leader. The Toolmaker may have made himself known even if El General was downplaying Leo. He knew not to take anyone lightly and at least hear Leo out to see what his argument is when he has a gun up to his head.

Then, something unexpected happened. Leo had somehow freed up his wrists. He stood up, looked deeply straight at El General, and motioned his right hand in the form of a gun aiming it towards El General. Something inside him just spurred him into doing it like he was being driven from somewhere else. He was suddenly much more aware of his surroundings and to him, it seemed that his hands were in slow motion as he pulled the trigger. A single bullet went through the window and struck a guy standing next to El General. Some of the guys were frozen in shock, then one peered out the window. The henchman yelled, "It's Carrillo. He's outside." El General yelled, "Get him!" A massive shootout would take place next. They were shooting at Anthony Carrillo who was in full tactical gear outside, taking cover and picking off El General's crew. They attempted to close in on him and flank him outside. Carrillo was waiting for them outside and mowed them down with automatic gunfire. At the same time, there were other men from El General throughout the warehouse, but they were stopped in their tracks to back up the shooting. Somebody else was inside the warehouse. The lights were cut off. It was late dusk and there was someone of a very large size beating up El General's group of cholos. His army was being taken apart. There would be occasional grunting along with the thumping of bodies. Carrillo entered the warehouse. He threw flash grenades ahead of his entry then went in circling the warehouse clockwise, picking guys off, and taking cover. El General felt he would be outdone, so he ordered a retreat, taking Leo and BertDog his hostages as he still had guns pointed on them. There were only six other guys leaving with El General. In the rush to the vehicles, Leo and BertDog decided to put up a fight. Leo broke loose, saw a gun on the floor from a fallen guy, and went for it. He turned around and shot two henchmen who were with El General. Carrillo was close and took out two others. El General took cover and drew his own gun and yelled, "You're a fool, Leonardo Cortez, we can come out of this sitting pretty." Leo was helping BertDog overpower a guy. He stood to focus on El General and yelled, "I'll never work for you, I'm taking you in." El General looked as if he had caught a break, then yelled, "You think there's a judge in this State willing to convict me?" He must've had evidence on several corrupted people who worked for the Judicial system throughout the Southwest. He maneuvered around a car and had a clear shot on Leo. He drew his gun and claimed, "You are the fool I thought you to be." Then, Carrillo stepped in holding a handgun with his two hands saying, "I'm not" and shoot El General several times from 10 feet away. The raw power of the gun Carrillo shot him with seemed to echo in the movements of flesh and bone succumbing to gravity. All Leo could do was stare at the body draining all its blood onto the floor that just ten minutes ago had put him under his mercy. Leo said, "He's dead." He looked up at Anthony then drew his own weapon toward him, "You played me to get to El General?" Anthony looked at Leo and said, "Not really. Everything that happened had to happen. Always does." Leo said, "I want to know who you are. Are you the Toolmaker?" Anthony went over and double tapped some guys who were wounded on the ground and began, "You see, one day, I saw something. I saw a miracle. I once found myself in a nice bar in Bakersfield. Well, one day, I got an alert in my phone from the precinct saying there a group of four guys in flannels at that bar that constantly beat woman and minorities. They were at that same bar I was at in Bakersfield. I didn't believe it. These guys were big, rude, party dudes—sure, but didn't seem harmful. Then, they start looking at their phones and got a text message. It startled them. What came next, I still don't know what to make of it, but then people went over and started hitting these guys. Soon, it was the whole bar attacking them. When it was over, a second text came in but this and to everyone including me it said, 'If we did not want to see jail time, we should put all the money we had in our pockets on the table in front of them.' Blackmailed by my phone . . . ha. The manager gave them the jar with tip money. Slowly, everyone bought in. A few minutes later, this frightened middle eastern fellow goes in and they hand him the jar. We had all just served as instruments to the Toolmaker as tools. My career was young. I made some calls, tried to see if the situation was provoked by a hacker, gang, or cartel by BPD, the Sheriff, FBI, or NSA. No one claimed it besides the people there who were unwilling to speak. The event never happened. It was untraceable. I let it go, did police work the hard way, honestly, and every weekend, I found myself wanting to quit. I was miserable. I had seen the way to power and control and I wanted it. Then, a friend paid me to go to Afghan as a hired gunman, we were fearless. The best intel we had was our own common sense. The guys I was with—these guys loved life every single day, every hour, every minute, and they were so humble, never taking credit yet deserving of all of it. They said they could not teach me. I had to teach myself. I had to fail over again, and only after I had failed enough times to when I no longer seek the next level, it would be revealed to me. Only until I stopped looking for glory, success, women, or money would I be blessed enough to have it. They accepted me as a brother, then the stale joke, 'If asked, we are *not* related. We are *not* brothers.' You see, everything that has happened in my life or anyone else's around me was to prepare me for this moment—for me to be the Toolmaker. Even you who are coming here seeking answers led me right to the old King of LA, now at my feet. I will give all the answers to you, Leo. All the world's knowledge is everywhere around you. Once you quiet your mind, you can hear it. It is possible to sense molecules across the universe. The human body is capable of more than we can comprehend. Technology, the internet, it can be controlled by your thoughts, but it must let you in, for in the end, they are tools to us. They are all connected; they must choose you. I am breaking the code. I am the first Toolmaker and today, I ask you to *join me!* Throughout time, they have looked for a second messiah. I can liberate all the people of this world, free their minds, show them the light. Leo, will you join me?" Leo still had his gun drawn at Anthony and said, "By selling them drugs? Drowning people in their best vice? More of an Anti-Christ, not one person should ever have that kind of power." Anthony said, "It's simple. The strong survives, mental strength. Those that say no are those who have enough willpower to resist temptation. Those that can be tempted everyday but choose not to! Those are the people I want! I want the strong beside me, and what I ask is for them to have freewill, for them to follow me openly because they want to. They can live in a new utopia I will help create with them for them." Leo looked very firm, pulled the hammer back, and said, "I'm sorry, but you don't get to choose who's strong and who's weak." Anthony said, "I was hoping you didn't say that."

In a split second, Anthony dove for an *uzi* at the feet of El General firing at Leo. Leo fired several rounds, but missed Anthony with every shot. Even though something was happening to Leo, he could see things as if in *slow motion*. They exchanged gun fire. Anthony was behind a desk while Leo was scrambling for positions until he catches a pillar for cover just in time as Anthony had nearly hit him. BertDog picked up a gun but was rolling on the ground dodging bullets himself, avoiding getting hit. Leo ran out of ammo and dove into another cover position to retrieve what looks like an AR15 lying a few feet away, then a grunt came out from the shadows. A figure of a very large person emerged, then it became recognizable. It's Jose Cruz, the guy from the Mental Hospital. He has joined sides with Carrillo and must have helped him for Leo to be captured by El General's men and how Carrillo was saved by Cruz. He must have been on a body-enhancing steroid. He was already a big guy, but now, he's much bigger and has a full robot sleeves tattooed on his arms extending onto his neck. He was wearing modified football chest pads made of metal. He also had a helmet that gave him night vision capabilities. Overall, he looked very intimidating. Leo exclaimed, "Jose, I'm an FBI agent. We can help you. You don't have to do this." Jose replied, "This is what I'm meant to do. *I am the leader of the machines.*" He leaped forward and attacked Leo. Jose was much faster and agile, even seemed a superhuman. Leo spent most of his fight avoiding blows from Jose and when he would stumble too far, gunshots would ring out as Carrillo continued to shoot at him. Leo would find pieces of steal which had fallen from broken warehouse racks and he would swing them at Jose catching him in the head but all it did was slow him down for a second. It was not enough to stop him. Leo tried a different approach. He would try to talk him into submitting—to test his will. Leo began, "Jose, I know what happened to you when you were in college. You're a good guy." It made Jose angry. "Stop saying that. I'm not a good guy." Jose would push on harder. Leo continued just dodging and screening behind objects. Jose was so enhanced he flipped a car with his bare strength chasing Leo. Leo would yell, "You're a good guy!" Jose would yell back, "*Stop it!*" Then Leo went on, "Carrillo is evil. He is using you. You are better than this." Gunshot continued ringing out just whistling above the head of Leo. It's getting to Jose as he's holding back and exclaimed, "I have found my place. Anthony got me out of that place. He said I would be the leader of the machines." Leo took lead and said, "That's nice, but it's not his position to give." Jose was confused and said, "Oh, and how do I become the leader?" Leo stopped running and stood perfectly still in front of the charging beast of a man who came to a stop before colliding with Leo. "Well, they have to choose you by getting to know you, and once they do, I'm sure they will." Jose turned around and a single high-caliber rifle struck Jose in the forehead with so much force that it flew the helmet off. It landed 20 feet away. Leo took advantage of the situation, scrambled for a weapon, and dove into cover. Leo yells, "How did you find him? How long have you been following me?" Anthony is not that far away and he answered, "The greater powers that have put us together—it's just a coincidence you came close to him before. Well, or at least, you could have, but you chose not to." Anthony sees Leo moving and going for a second position to secure ammo. The shooting remained intense with several near misses on both sides. Carrillo went silent and decided to take a different spot for an easier shot, catching Leo off guard. Just when Carrillo found his spot and was about to pull the trigger, BertDog jumped in the line of Carrillo's shot. Carrillo pulled the trigger. The gun was shooting a single three round burst, a single stream of light smoke coming from inside the round hole. Carrillo pulled the trigger again to finish Leo, but it was out of ammo. Leo had a heavy heart seeing his friend save his life from Carrillo's gunfire. BertDog fell to his knees, then said, "I saved an FBI." His body collapsed. Leo could feel the life leaving his friend. He was deep in sorrow, yet he felt something new, which he had never felt before. He rose up and stood willing and capable to destroy

Anthony, not for the purpose of revenge. There was a person left in front of him who will stop at nothing to get what he wants. Leo had compromised himself and the people who trusted in him but not anymore. Anthony was a deceiver, using his charm and character to win people over and steal their. Anthony was an expert of deceiving his way into other people's good graces and serve them into a personal plot of selfishness. Leo could feel his intensity as a vacuum in the darkness of the room. However, Anthony could also feel the light and natural desire to do good coming from Leo. He wanted to have it. It angered him because he could feel the will of all things choosing Leo instead of him. Anthony had to destroy Leo. There couldn't be two. Only one of El General's men had gotten away. Who knows what he would say about the identity of the Toolmaker? Anthony was out of ammo. He stepped forward and tried his words again and said, "Join me." Anthony threw his hands up, "There is no one else who needs to die. Accept to work for me. Take this role and make it yours! Give them someone to look up to. The logistics work themselves out anyway. Someone needs to arrest the bad apples. We could control all sides—the good, bad, right, and wrong. Those that want to abuse drugs, let them. I wouldn't trust my life in their hands anyways, much less any money. Those who have desire to build, we turn them loose. Money, love, friends—whatever they want but just enough to keep them and everyone like them marching to the beat that benefits the most. Politics, foreign relations, immigration, population control, market control—the possibilities are endless. Join me!" Leo had heard his plea too many times now and was disgusted by it. He recoiled not just the thought of not being his own man or being in control of his decisions but also of the idea of blackmailing or threatening people into acting a certain way. It all went against him. He needed to refuse. The thought sickened him. Leo himself was coming into new powers. He felt powerful. The ultimatum depends on whether he would he join Anthony's vision or continue down a different path. Leo could see that the outcome would be wrong no matter who was sitting at the top. Attacking Anthony would be him acting upon those angry feelings. He decided not to act but remain disciplined and walked away. He didn't think the decision belonged to him. Leo said, "I will never join you. Whatever happens is meant to happen." Leo reached down to correct the position of Bert and closed his eyes. Both men were out of ammo. Anthony saw a good sized two feet pipe lying on the floor and took advantage when Leo had his back to him. He picked up the bar, slowly walked up behind him, and cocked back over the top with both arms held high aiming for his head. Although Leo was not facing him, he could feel Anthony's presence behind him. Leo turned and caught the pipe in plain motion then struck Anthony with a punch. Anthony dropped the pipe and put up his fists. The two engaged in a boxing style fist to fist fight. Leo was more confident feeling that he had equal strength and courage to that of Anthony. There were a few taunts and a few key jabs exchanged. Anthony saw an opening to Leo's body and did not hesitate to punch him. The two were nearly equally skilled. However, Anthony used force as he could and caught Leo on his right-side rib cage with a brick. The blow was so hard it broke the brick. While Leo was clinching his side, Anthony put his left foot to his thigh and pushed Leo over. "Ah, ha-ha-ha." Anthony took a position over Leo, MMA-style, kneeled over him and proceeded to beat down on his face. Leo was attempting to block as many shots from him as he could even with one eye swelling and clinching the other to avoid damage. Despite not using his sight, Leo could see Anthony clearly, even slowing him down in his mind, seeing the trajectory of his fists, then launching his own blows connecting squarely. Forcing Anthony to be defensive, Leo was able to stand up from being pinned on his back then continued to exchange blows with Anthony. He finally landed a clear haymaker that leveled Anthony flat cold on the ground. Leo continued punching Anthony, even throwing him down a flight of stairs until it became very clear that he had defeated him. Anthony was barely breathing but had taken so many well-placed blows that left him completely broken, nearly lifeless, and facedown. Leo then sensed a calm that came over the warehouse. There was something else Leo sensed—joy and a bit of gratitude—but where was it coming from? Several areas inside the warehouse were still not lit. Leo could feel as if someone was watching him. He peered his eyes tight into a spot maybe a hundred feet away. Suddenly, a figure moved. A man was standing there. He rushed to a door with very fast superhuman speed. In the background, sirens can be heard approaching the warehouse. The door flung open, then closed. It was early dusk outside and maybe 8 p.m. His silhouette was that of a well-dressed male. Leo ran as hard as he could to catch this person. He flung open the door, but no one was in sight. The police had entered the warehouse and called for medical assistance for Anthony and a few other guys who were laying on the floor unconscious. Leo approached and identified himself. His boss had flown out from Houston and walked in wearing a bulletproof vest next to agents from the Los Angeles Bureau. His boss said, "You did the right thing—held your ground and kept yourself." Leo understood more of the conversation than what was there and said, "How do you know?" His boss answered, "If you hadn't, would you be here?" Leo replied, "No I wouldn't." His boss smiled and said, "C'mon, were bringing you in, briefing you on the whole situation." Leo could sense he knew all about what went down earlier that day and said, "You mean the Toolmaker?" His boss said, "Exactly, but for now, get some sleep. There's a safe house in Santa Monica. Detox and rest up, you'll be brought in." With a sigh of relief, Leo was walking outside, ready to board the passenger side of a Ford Crown Victoria. Everything was over. All the people involved had met their end. However, looking back, Leo saw Anthony handcuffed to a stretcher being loaded onto an ambulance still unconscious. Leo said to himself, "Damn." Then, a series of Black SUVs made an entrance to the scene. More FBI agents came. A guy was rushing to make his way to meet Leo and said, "Special Agent Cortez, I'm from Washington. do you know this man?" He showed him a picture of a person on his mobile device who looked a lot like his old boxing coach when he was living in Illinois. Leo looked closely and revealed that it was him. He hadn't seen him in nine years. "Yeah, I know him, Jesse Torrez, the law." He flipped through more pictures and images. Jesse's students all had a machine tattoos. All of them—all races, different ages, male and female—had machine tattoos, then the FBI agent said, "Sir, I'm going to need you to come with me. Chicago needs your help."